HAUNTED NEW ORLEANS

HAUNTED NEW ORLEANS

Southern Spirits, Garden District
Ghosts, and Vampire Venues

Retold by Bonnye Stuart

Guilford, Connecticut

Copyright © 2012 by Morris Book Publishing, LLC

Text design: Sheryl P. Kober
Editor: Tracee Williams
Project editor: Lauren Brancato
Layout: Sue Murray

Library of Congress Cataloging-in-Publication Data

Stuart, Bonnye E.
  Haunted New Orleans : Southern spirits, garden district ghosts, and vampire venues / retold by Bonnye Stuart.
     p. cm.
  Includes bibliographical references.
  ISBN 978-0-7627-6437-2
  1. Haunted places—Louisiana—New Orleans. I. Title.
  BF1472.U6S779 2012
  133.109763'35—dc23

                                                                2012008252

Printed in the United States of America

10 9 8 7 6 5 4 3 2 1

To wondrous spirits of my own past,
may they rest in peace and serenity

CONTENTS

ACKNOWLEDGMENTS

This manuscript was due on All Saints' Day, an important religious holiday celebrated by New Orleans Catholics. Its significance as a way to connect with those who have the ear of God crosses all geographic, economic, social, and political boundaries. Even sports fans celebrate the Saints. We pray to those who have achieved perfection and beatification to help us here on earth. We pray for health, wealth, good fortune, and a winning season.

On All Saints' Day, November 1, many people visit cemeteries to pray for special help from loved ones who are thought to have entered the Pearly Gates. But for some New Orleanians November 2 is the day they set aside to visit the cemetery. On the Feast of All Souls or, more officially, the Commemoration of All the Faithful Departed, people don't pray *to* loved ones, but rather *for* them. Also called the Day of the Dead, this day is dedicated to those souls who have passed over but remain in purgatory to atone for sins committed on earth. They can be helped by earthly prayers, novenas, intercessions, and Masses in their honor. On this day New Orleanians visit the grave sites of their loved ones and pray that their souls may rest in peace. It's also the time to spruce up the place. Family members bring "fresh" flowers, both real and plastic, vases are cleaned of mold and mildew, weeds are pulled, debris is removed, and Mardi Gras beads are often hung on tombstones to give those buried there something to look forward to after the cold, damp winter days are over. No wonder that New Orleans has earned the title of "the most haunted city in the world." Praying for Souls, petitioning Saints, speaking to the Dead, celebrating festivals with family and friends entombed in aboveground mausoleums, an occasional *gris-gris* curse when things aren't going so well—it's all part of life in New Orleans. When I opened my Facebook page on All Souls' Day, I had two pictures of my mother's grave site, one from each of my sisters. The flowers were beautiful and plentiful and, yes, there were new doubloons and Mardi Gras beads decorating the area.

I would like to acknowledge my city, New Orleans, for cultivating my long heritage within its loving arms. I am a ninth-generation New Orleanian, and the city's customs, folklore, mores, and superstitions are in my blood. I have visited, eaten at, imbibed at, stayed in, and celebrated many of the places in this book. Some of the stories include real details of true occurrences; only those closest to our family will recognize them. I'm not sure I believe all the tales I came across, but I do know that in New Orleans there are often and everywhere unexplainable happenings and odd sightings.

I would like to thank all the writers of all the stories, books, histories, websites, journals, and newspaper articles that gave me such incredible information from which to extract these tales. Winthrop University has been a great help in getting books and articles for me from all over the country.

My deepest love and gratitude go to my immediate family, which is ever expanding: David, Ruby, Lilli, Elizabeth, Jeff, Jack, Tennyson, Jessica, Frank, Emily, Lauren, Braden, Christian, Jessica Lee, Kingston, and a baby boy on the way. There are others to thank, but the list is getting too long. You know who you are. You have supported me through the process and forgiven my negligence due to looming deadlines. Special thanks and love go to my husband, Laurence, who keeps all things going at home, reminds me to take my phone with me, and always has my coffee ready in the morning.

INTRODUCTION

"Do you agree that, when we speak of a ghost, we imply the preceding existence of something or someone corporeal? That is, something or someone having had a body before that thing or person achieved ghostliness? Yes or no?"

—*Seamus Deane,* Reading in the Dark

Romantic, carefree, spicy, eccentric, sultry, mysterious, garish, wondrous, exotic, fabulous, strange, extraordinary, eerie, quaint, and spooky, this is New Orleans. The list could be, should be, longer. Time often clouds memory, but early descriptions of the city, her people, and her long and tumultuous past are recorded in numerous history books, letters, and legal documents. Over the past three hundred years, the city herself has endured, undulating through each successive wave of change, whether individual, governmental, or natural, to emerge strong and vibrant. Many forces have tried, some successfully and others unsuccessfully, to alter the unique New Orleans way of life. The words of the living have recorded her story, but many spirits have stayed behind to relive the past in the present. They have been around since the beginning.

The city's early French history was rooted in staunch Catholicism and reinforced by the Spanish. Praying to saints, long dead, to intercede for the living was a consolation for the unfortunate. When African slaves and Haitian refugees arrived, they brought with them religious practices, many based on superstition and voodoo. A Creole culture developed, drawing on the best and worst of both worlds as believers sought to alleviate pain and suffering.

And New Orleans was a place of much suffering. Soggy, mosquito-infested swamps, deadly reptiles, intense heat, and rampant disease were a part of life for the early settlers. Sister Madeleine Hachard, one of the first Ursuline nuns to arrive in the colony, writes, "From these woods come clouds of mosquitoes, gnats, and another kind of fly. . . . These wicked animals bite without mercy." These "wicked animals" brought malaria and yellow fever and death. Many died too young, and families fearing for their children turned to prayer and incantation. African slaves beseeched voodoo priests and priestesses for delivery from cruelty, forced separation from loved ones, and tortured death. Hurricanes, fires, epidemics, hardship, New Orleans experienced it all. The city was always wet—water lurking below the surface or floodwaters inundating her streets.

Somehow in New Orleans the dead got all mixed up with the living; superstition became part of religion. A Catholic tradition of building an altar to celebrate St. Joseph's help with famine is juxtaposed with the practice of burying a small statue of St. Joseph upside down in the front yard to help sell a house. It's perhaps easy to see why things got so jumbled. The dead are aboveground in cemeteries where they are looked after in their homelike mausoleums called "Cities of the Dead." Graves are decorated with flowers, Mardi Gras beads, St. Patrick shamrocks, and "lucky" fava beans. Sacred religious holidays such as St. John's Eve, All Souls' Day, and All Saints' Day celebrate the spirit world as if the dead are still among the living. The knowledge of indigenous healing herbs led to charms and amulets that could protect oneself or harm others. Voodoo Queen Marie Laveau preyed on these superstitions to garner a loyal following. Her name is still evoked today when someone or something needs to be "taken care of."

New Orleanians grow up accepting ghosts, spirits, even apparitions as part of life. It was through Louisiana Voodoo that such terms as *gris-gris* and *voodoo dolls* were introduced into the American lexicon. Voodoo dolls are playthings of little girls. Putting a hex on someone is as common, and easy, as saying good-bye. And what New Orleans native hasn't put the gris-gris on a plan she wanted fouled or an opponent he wanted to beat?

Catholicism says that the souls of unbaptized children float in limbo, and so, too, do those who had not finished their work on earth. The idea that spirits, both good and evil, stay behind trapped between worlds surfaced very early, as evidenced by Père Dagobert, the Capuchin monk who defied authority in 1769 and who still sings in Jackson Square; the souls of yellow fever victims that haunt the Bourbon Orleans; and the tormented spirit of Madame Lalaurie who lingers restless and guilt-ridden. The dark side of the Crescent City's history is documented in written letters and oral stories in which brutality, ruthlessness, inhumanity, and barbarity reigned and the idea that the powerless could change their fate or punish an oppressor, if not in this world, then in the next, became a workable belief.

More than 150 years after its founding, the city was still struggling with disease and pestilence. In 1881, Mark Twain, referring to New Orleans, wrote that "the deep, troughlike gutters along the curbstones were still half full of reposeful water with a dusty surface . . . the great blocks of austerely plain commercial houses were as dusty-looking as ever." New Orleans, a blend of beauty and ruin, has known great splendor and cruel death. The city has never left the past behind, choosing instead to live in harmony with the spirits of other worlds. Generations of native New Orleanians don't want to leave, and never will. They think New Orleans is the best place on earth, and they understand why ghosts, phantoms, and spirits want to stay, too.

Part One

HAUNTED HOTELS AND HOUSES

New Orleans is one of the most frequented vacation destinations in the United States. The mysterious, old, quaint, rowdy city attracts an eclectic crowd of history buffs interested in long-ago people and places and noisy revelers looking to "pass a good time." The Crescent City has something for everyone, including many welcoming, and not so welcoming, resident ghosts and spirits from the past.

Interesting and haunted places to stay in New Orleans are easily found on vacation sites. We will visit only a few of the many that have intriguing stories or tall tales to tell. The ghosts at the palatial Royal Orleans, the Bourbon Orleans, the Dauphine Orleans, and the Hotel Monteleone enjoy an atmosphere of Southern opulence, while the Hotel Provincial, the Andrew Jackson, and the Columns Hotel cater to lingering spirits who want a more intimate setting. The Beauregard-Keyes, Lalaurie, Griffon, and Sultan Houses offer visitors a chance to imagine for a moment the past glories and sinful imperfections of a bustling river port.

So come for Mardi Gras or the Jazz Fest, ride a steamboat up the Mississippi River or a streetcar down St. Charles Avenue. Just come! But be careful when you book your hotel—haunted spirits may be waiting to escort you down the hall to your room or even tuck you into your bed at night.

Chapter 1

Desolate Spirits at Hotel Provincial

Civil War soldiers fought for a mighty cause, but the human cost was high and casualties were plentiful. From the battlefields around New Orleans, up the Mississippi River Valley and as far away as Natchez, Mississippi, and the panhandle of Florida, wounded men in dire need of medical care flooded into the city, now occupied by Yankee troops. Hospitals were overextended and medical staffs exhausted. A temporary hospital was set up in a spacious boardinghouse and connecting coffee shop in the French Quarter to afford many patients a quiet respite from their troubles, either through healing . . . or death. But when the war ended and Reconstruction in the South began, not all patients vacated the premises. Today the site of this Civil War hospital is home to the Hotel Provincial where, some say, the maimed and broken bodies of tortured souls still roam the halls and occasionally reach out to guests for help.

Mark and Cate were looking forward to spending their honeymoon in New Orleans, the "City That Care Forgot." But they would not soon forget their experiences at the Hotel Provincial. When the cab driver let them off at 1024 Rue Chartres in the shadow of the Mississippi River, Mark noticed a peculiarly curled smile on the face of the heavy man with the Cajun accent unloading the couple's meager luggage from the taxi's trunk. *Well,* Mark thought, *he's just amused that we're a newly wed couple from the country visiting the big city for the first time.*

Marko, as his friends called him, felt quite the lucky man as he swaggered from the main street, through the private inner courtyard of the Hotel Provincial, and walked haughtily up to the front desk to sign in for the first time as husband and wife. Cate was mesmerized by the sultry Old World ambience of the hotel, looking right and left, agog at the beautiful tropical plants and fig ivy espaliers crawling up the exposed brick walls. Marko reached for Cate's hand, telling her their room was on the second floor of Building 500.

The couple noted the inviting swimming pool and lush gardens as they made their way across the courtyard. Their room, though small, was just what they expected from the quaint old hostelry in the heart of the French Quarter. Southern antiques adorned the room, and as they looked out upon the romantic city, they could almost see the mighty Mississippi River winding its way just beyond the levee.

Marko strode over to his new wife, who was closing the door after the bellhop. He put his arms around her, but suddenly she turned to him with startled eyes. Later he was to remember the rush of love he felt for her; she had the biggest, roundest, and bluest eyes he had ever seen. She stared hard at her new husband. "What's he doing here?" she blurted. Marko scanned the room, then looked at the door; it was shut, and they were alone. "What are you talking about, Cate?" Her face was ghostly white. "That man with the bloody . . ."

The Hotel Provincial is a charming and graceful hotel composed of five buildings with a long and colorful past. Building 100 and Building 200 are built on land granted in 1725 from Louis XV, king of France, to Louis Boucher de Granpre, lieutenant to Jean-Baptiste Le Moyne de Bienville, one of the founders of New Orleans. The property changed hands several times as fortunes were won and lost—from Chevalier Jean Lavillebeuvre, an Indian agent of the French colony who owned it from 1780 to 1797, to the Lauran and Roque families, who bought and developed the land throughout the 1800s. At the turn of the twentieth century, as industrialization found its way across the Mason-Dixon Line, from northern metro centers to the sleepy southern city lounging languidly in the crescent-shaped curve of the Mississippi River, the property was sold to the French Market Ice Company in 1903 as a commercial venture. After a devastating fire in 1958 destroyed the ice company, the Dupepe family bought the property, and the first buildings that would become the Hotel Provincial were completed in 1961. As the success of their hotel grew, the family began to expand by buying properties and buildings close by.

Building 300 began as land that, since the founding of the city, had served as medicinal herb gardens for the nearby military Royal Hospital. Sister Francis Xavier Hebert, an Ursuline nun, planted herbs for teas, infusions, and distillates in an ample garden at the rear of the convent. Her efforts were supported by a treaty between the religious order of Ursulines and the Company of the Indies that stated: "Sufficient ground, adjoining the house shall be granted . . . both to erect there the new buildings of which there may be need and to make a garden for the religious." The property was bought during the eighteenth century by the archbishop of New Orleans, who sold it in 1820. By 1825 the tract was the site of a spacious city house with slave quarters in the rear. Restoration of Building 300 of the Hotel Provincial was completed in 1967.

Building 400 began as a retail store downstairs and living quarters upstairs in the 1830s Creole tradition. The site was home to a commercial business for many years and was a hardware store when it was purchased and restored in 1964 as part of the Hotel Provincial. Probably the most interesting parcel of land is that on which now stands Building 500. The Royal Hospital was erected by order of Louis XV in 1722 on the site, and this small military hospital came under the domain of the Ursuline nuns when they arrived from France in 1727 in service to the city and its residents. This facility welcomed both American and British soldiers who had been wounded during the 1815 Battle of New Orleans, which ended the War of 1812. Patients were nursed to health with Sister Xavier's medicinal herbal concoctions of catnip, rosemary, sweet marjoram, sage, pot marigold, and pennyroyal.

In 1831, Archbishop Leon de Necke sold the property and the now quite old hospital to Antoine Abat, who in turn sold it to Dominique Seghers, an attorney who demolished the aging structure and built two imposing houses in its stead. In 1848 the mansions were bought, united by a hallway, and turned into a boardinghouse, retail space, and coffee shop by Françoise Sambola. By the 1860s New Orleans was embroiled in the throes of the Civil War, and in April 1862 the city surrendered to a Union fleet with minimal resistance. Federal troops occupied the city, and the Medical College was closed for the duration of the war, because many student doctors and faculty had joined the Confederate army. Severe physician shortages resulted. With fighting all around and the city pressed to the wall with war causalities, the capacious structures of the boardinghouse and coffee shop were commandeered, by order of Major General Benjamin Butler, the federal military governor, as an adjunct military hospital for wounded and dying soldiers. Doctors were stretched to their limits as nurses rushed from patient to patient seeing to their wounds and dying wishes.

It is Building 500 that guests and hotel staff say is most haunted. Over the years many stories have been reported by hotel visitors and employees alike. This doesn't seem too unusual for a property that has seen the mayhem of two wars and its share of suffering and death. Guests entering their rooms have reported seeing soldiers with bandaged heads moaning in pain. One woman complained that she had been grabbed and pulled from her bed by something or someone unseen. A security guard claimed to have seen an entire hospital floor of nurses rushing around administering to wounded Confederate soldiers as the elevator opened onto the second floor of Building 500. There are stories of phantom whispers, doors opening and shutting by themselves, freezing cold areas, and steaming hot spots. Guests and staff have described soldiers with crutches and arms in slings roaming the hotel grounds, in the courtyard as well as the lobby, and medical staff with bloodied aprons and medical garb. Hotel maids have often complained of pools of blood on the floor that appear and subsequently disappear. Others report seeing soiled towels in their bathrooms turn into bloody bandages and bedding. Guests recall hearing organ music playing throughout Building 500, but no organ is on the premises. The building once housed an organ, but that was given to a local church just after the Civil War. In 1874, almost a decade after the Civil War ended, both the boardinghouse and the cafe that had served as the military hospital for Confederate soldiers burned to the ground in a tragic fire of unknown cause. The present building was built soon after the fire and in 1916 became the headquarters of the Reuter Seed Company. A bellman showing a couple their room shared a story about the room's ghost, a man in a medaled military uniform who often visits guests. The couple reported seeing the man, who looked intently in their eyes, then disappeared. They said they captured the man's image on film. Another soldier apparently likes oldies music and will change the radio in the room from whichever station it is on to his favorite station, WTIX. A séance was held to document the recurring phenomenon. The man materialized, spoke to those assembled in the room, and then disappeared through the wall. When tape recorders played back the session, the man could be heard asking someone to please tell Diane he had to go. Several images on film and videotape are said to have captured the stern face of a man in uniform and the flash of his military medals. The Dupepe family bought the building in 1969, completing the properties that make up the charming Hotel Provincial complex. Buildings 100 and 200 are decorated in nineteenth-century New Orleans style. Buildings 300 and 400 have been returned to their original 1820s architectural style. The old herb garden of the Ursuline Convent continues to flourish and was featured on the PBS program *Victory Garden*. Building 500, where you will want to stay if you are interested in meeting a ghost, is today an authentic restoration of the original 1875 structure. Guests flock to this popular French Quarter hotel, and recent blogs have described bloodstains that mysteriously appear and disappear on the bedding and disembodied spirits floating around the grounds. The Hotel

Provincial ghosts are not afraid of having their pictures taken as the Haunted History Tour in New Orleans strolls through the lobby, replete with distressing memories and anguished spirits of the old hospital corridors. So many people who experienced trauma and death on these premises have chosen to linger here that there are no specific names to associate with the hauntings, but the Hotel Provincial is regarded as one of the most haunted hotels in New Orleans.

Cate had not heard any of these stories when she turned to her new husband for consolation. She explained that she had seen a young soldier, in a tattered uniform, with his limbs wrapped in bloody bandages. She described in detail how the blood ran from his arms to the floor. "It was so real," she repeated over and over again. Marko tried to comfort her. He turned the radio to a classical station. This will soothe her, he said to himself as he started to run a bath for his agitated wife. In seconds, the lyrical sonata stopped, the station changed frequencies on its own, and Marko heard, "Welcome back to your oldies rock station, WTIX-FM at 94.3 on the dial." Now it was Marko's turn to stare wide-eyed and apprehensively around his honeymoon suite.

Chapter 2

Andrew Jackson, a Hero Lives On

New Orleans is indebted to Andrew Jackson, hero of the Battle of New Orleans. It seems he still enjoys his celebrated nineteenth-century reputation and fame as many people have reported that his ghost frequents several places throughout the city even today.

Frank surprised his wife, Jessica, with a trip to New Orleans . . . away from the children. They had two daughters, ages ten and eight, and a four-year-old son who were involved in all sorts of activities from volunteering at the local SPCA to basketball and soccer. This vacation would be a quiet getaway, a chance to unwind, take long walks through the French Quarter, visit a museum or two, and eat wonderful food. After checking in at the Andrew Jackson Hotel on Royal Street, the couple went directly to room 111, at the back, facing the courtyard, to deposit their luggage and get out on the town. The quaint hotel had beautiful period furnishings as advertised. Frank was proud that he had made all the arrangements himself. While Jessica changed clothes, Frank looked through the city guide on the desk for things to do and see. It was almost dinnertime, and he was looking forward to a great meal at a Cajun restaurant.

"Jess," Frank called out. "Listen to what they say about our hotel. 'The Andrew Jackson is located in the heart of the French Quarter, and many say that it is haunted.' That's funny, isn't it? You don't think the hotel is haunted, do you?"

Jessica was ready to enjoy her weekend and didn't want to spend time dwelling on "haunted" places. "Of course not," she said. "It's just a gimmick to attract tourists." She walked to the centuries-old wrought-iron balcony overlooking Royal Street and the French Quarter. "Let's go find a place for dinner."

The couple left the hotel behind and returned exhausted a few hours later; they had been up since 6 a.m. making sure Nana was set to handle all the weekend activities with the children. Looking forward to a good rest before hitting the streets again the next day, they climbed into bed and quickly drifted off to sleep. But sleep did not linger long. Of all things they were awakened by the cries and commotion of young children playing in the courtyard below their window while another child was bouncing a ball against the wall of their room. How could this be happening on their weekend away from the kids? Frank reached for the phone and dialed the front desk. The night clerk did not seem concerned—he said he had heard the complaints before.

The history of the site where the Andrew Jackson Hotel sits today goes back more than two hundred years. It seems that "layers" of ghosts haunt this place, each connected to lives lived in the distant past. Stories vary in details, though not in substance. The late 1700s brought much death and destruction to the fledgling city. To help with the children who were abandoned and left behind due to sickness and disease, yellow fever epidemics, lack of resources, fire, and floods, an all-boys orphanage and public school was built at 919 Royal Street until it, too, was destroyed. Some say a horrific fire was started as the orphanage swayed and rattled in a fierce hurricane that swept in from the Gulf of Mexico at the end of August 1794. The storm had devastated Cuba, and as the surge moved inland, it brought unprecedented hail and nine hours of tormenting winds that destroyed lives, cattle, and crops. Ships were overturned in the Mississippi River, and Governor Carondelet was forced to ask for financial assistance for the affected area.

Others blame the devastation of the orphanage on the great fire, six months later in December 1794, that burned so many homes and city buildings. In any case, it was recorded that fire killed at least five young boys as the orphanage went up in flames. These children's ghosts have never left the orphanage site. They romp around the cast-iron fountain and play in the deserted courtyard. The children roam the hallways of the hotel, calling out loudly to each other. The boys seem to like playing in the middle of the night, perhaps because they can, now that no bedtime can be enforced. Guests have reported loud laughter and playful shrieking as the young boys pass in and out and through walls. Boisterous specters zip through the lobby unchecked.

The manager gets calls from guests asking him to keep the children quiet when no children are in the hotel. He says the calls, usually between two and three in the morning, most often come from the guest rooms at the back of the hotel. He has seen the ghosts of children himself and understands the complaints. He tells of seeing the fleeting shadows of children disappearing into walls and the tops of the heads of the perished children over his lobby counter as they approached the front desk. Then, poof, they were gone.

After the ashes of the orphanage were cleared and long before the hotel was constructed, the first courthouse was built to serve as the US District Court for the territory. A disheartened ghost has been seen in the corner of the courtyard. Only part of the specter can be seen, with his head bowed and hands tied behind his back as if ready to be led away to a deadly fate. People report the sad, gloomy spirit of a hopeless man. Perhaps he was convicted of a crime he did or didn't commit; perhaps he was hanged on the very spot where he stands. No one knows, but he is there, sulking in the shadows.

The most famous ghost haunting the hotel is Andrew Jackson himself. Guests report seeing the ghostly figure of General Jackson walking through the hotel. Jackson was the hero of New Orleans in the War of 1812 when the United States fought Great Britain. By 1814, following his success as a military commander in the Battle of Horseshoe Bend, Jackson was promoted to major general in command of the southern frontier. To thwart plans of a British attack on New Orleans, a major gateway to the interior of the country, Jackson led a force of regulars, volunteers, militia, free blacks, and pirates to fortify the banks of the Mississippi River. On January 8, 1815, British General Sir Edward Pakenham led a frontal assault on Jackson's position. Jackson's men stood firm with artillery and rifle fire, stopping the advancing British army. The British casualties during this battle exceeded two thousand while Jackson suffered only thirteen dead and fifty-eight wounded and missing.

Neither side knew that the Treaty of Ghent ending the war had been signed two weeks earlier. Though the battle's outcome did not affect who won the war, the victory had great significance for the people of New Orleans. Jackson's low casualty number and the inspirational image of the American frontiersmen defeating hardened British veterans became legend. Jackson was a national hero. But even heroes have legal battles. Major General Andrew Jackson would end up being indicted for contempt of court and charged with obstruction of justice. After he had won the Battle of New Orleans, Jackson continued to maintain martial law in the city, ignoring news that a declaration of peace had been signed. Some citizens criticized Jackson for this, and Louis Louallier wrote an article in the local newspaper denouncing Jackson's policy of bringing people who were accused of a crime before a military tribunal instead of before a civilian court. Jackson had the writer arrested and imprisoned on charges of inciting mutiny and disaffection in the army. When US District Court Judge Dominick Hall ordered Jackson to free Louallier on the grounds that martial law was no longer in effect, Jackson refused. He then had the judge banished from the city. When martial law was lifted, Judge Hall returned to the courtroom and cited Jackson for contempt of court. According to the indictment, Jackson had "disrespectfully wrested from the clerk an original order of the honorable judge of this court, for the issuing of a writ of habeas corpus in the case of a certain Louis Louallier, then imprisoned by the said Major General Andrew Jackson." Jackson held Louallier in jail until official confirmation of the peace treaty was received. US Attorney John Dick indicted Jackson on a charge of obstruction of justice, incurred by his act of banishing Judge Hall. When Jackson appeared in court, he refused to answer the interrogatories and promptly received a fine of one thousand dollars, which he paid before leaving the court. Outside the courthouse, Jackson spoke to a large crowd that was shouting, "Vive le General Jackson!" He vowed to submit to the will of the court and the letter of the law. He was given a carriage ride through the city, stopping to greet citizens along the way. His supporters raised one thousand dollars to repay Jackson, but the general insisted the money be given to the widows and orphans of those who died in the Battle of New Orleans. It is said that Jackson's spirit still roams the very ground on which he pledged allegiance to the law and from which he was to go on to win the presidency of the United States. In 1844, Congress ordered the fine to be repaid to Jackson with interest ($2,700).

By the 1840s the notorious courthouse was no longer in operation, and by 1888 the building had been torn down. In its place a one-story boardinghouse was constructed with a Spanish Colonial red-tiled roof, an inner courtyard, and architectural motifs popular at the time. A second story was added later, and this structure remains today as the twenty-two-room Andrew Jackson Hotel.

The hotel is home to more playful ghosts. A young boy, not part of the earlier orphanage gang, haunts the second floor. It is reported that this boy, known only as Armand (or Armond), died here. Depending on the storyteller, he either jumped to his death or was thrown from the second-story balcony. Armand relishes waking up guests with childlike sounds or light, annoying touches. Some female guests have been awakened by a giggling little boy lightly tickling their feet from the foot of their bed. A few visitors have said they felt someone bouncing on their bed during the night. Armand also delights in pushing sleepers out of bed onto the floor. Guests have reported sensing an eerie presence in room 208, and it is not unusual for them to request a room change. They explain that they feel a strange sensation, as if they were not alone in the room. Lights go off and on at will, and faucets turn on by themselves. Guests have reported articles moved or disappearing altogether. Armand has been blamed for the harmless pranks played on visitors; the cleaning staff reluctantly and warily enters the room, and some won't go in at all.

The hotel is also haunted by a woman, whose presence can be felt in some rooms. She seems to be very interested in the particulars of the hotel. She has been seen straightening towels and fluffing pillows. She also cannot resist adjusting chairs to their original positions. This woman was perhaps a housekeeper or maybe the owner of the establishment. Housekeeping reports the feeling of someone watching over them from behind as they carry on their work. Guests have complained of doors opening and shutting by themselves and told tales of a woman who walks up and down the steps. On the staircase landing leading down to the first-floor lobby, guests have said they feel they are being watched, as if they aren't alone. The multiple ghosts seem to command their own space and coexist in the old building, living out lives that were in some way connected to the site. In 1965, the Andrew Jackson Hotel was listed on the National Register of Historic Places.

Frank finished talking to the night clerk and hung up the phone. "What did he say?" Jessica asked. "Is he going to quiet those kids?" Frank turned to Jessica. "Jess, the manager said there are no children registered in the hotel at all." Jessica closed her gaping mouth. "Oh? Well, I guess it will be just like home, then, won't it? We certainly know how to ignore playful commotion, ghosts or no ghosts. Let's get some rest. There's a lot I want to do tomorrow . . . without children!"

Chapter 3
The "Royal O"

Few buildings in New Orleans have witnessed as much historical drama as the old St. Louis Hotel. Maspero's nineteenth-century coffeehouse first stood on this site, and in a cramped upstairs storage area, slaves were held to be bought and sold like chattel on the auction block below. The coffeehouse below served as a literary meeting place for an influential cast of journalists and businessmen. La Bourse de Maspero was not where the Original Pierre Maspero's Food & Spirits is presently but was diagonally across the street on the St. Louis Hotel property, now the Omni Royal Orleans Hotel. The old St. Louis was a fabulous structure whose balloonlike central dome reached boldly toward the heavens. Paul Morphy's home, Napoleon House, and the French Market are within eyesight. Street names and numbers are not important to the spirits of the unforgettable characters who once lived, worked, played, suffered, plotted, dined, and died in this part of the Vieux Carré.

Elinor had planned a special surprise for her niece, Tennyson, and twin nephews, Braden and Kingston, to celebrate their birthdays, which were all in October. She would take them to the Sunday Jazz Brunch at the Omni Royal Orleans Hotel, known to New Orleanians as the "Royal O," for a culinary feast and entertainment by Sugar Bear and the Jazz Cats. After that she would take them to the St. Louis Cathedral; she wanted them to see where their parents had been married. Next they would stroll around Jackson Square, get their portraits drawn by one of the charcoal artists in the square, and, of course, indulge in some powdered sugar beignets at Café du Monde before heading home.

After parking the car, Elinor led the way to the Royal O; she was looking forward to some great food. She almost knew the menu by heart: Creole Cinnamon Fritters, Strawberries Esplanade, Eggs Sardou, Sweet Potato Bread Pudding. She had been there many times and had been promising to take the children. She was excited to see how impressed they were by the beautiful hotel. Arriving a little early for brunch, Elinor settled herself in one of the lush antique chairs in the lobby and told the children they could wander around a little as long as they stayed where she could see them. "And don't touch anything," she commanded. The boys immediately began playing on the beautiful marble steps leading from the mezzanine lobby to the ground floor, going up and down, up and down, never seeming to tire of the activity. They would hold the railing, or not, take the steps one at a time, then two at a time, then three. "Don't jump on the stairs," Elinor called out in anticipation of their next move. She scanned the area for Tennyson, who had sauntered over to one of the exotic dark statues and was running her fingers along the smooth surface. "Don't touch," Elinor called. Tennyson was hungry and didn't like waiting. She looked over at her two brothers now counting the steps. She was bored. She sat on a chair opposite a small antique table and began kicking at the bronze-capped legs. Elinor was about to reprimand her when Tennyson suddenly jumped out of the chair and dashed, screaming, over to Elinor. "Stop yelling," demanded Elinor, looking around at the gaping faces that seemed to pass judgment on a noisy child. "What's the matter?" she asked. Tennyson managed to stop screaming. The boys rushed over to see what was going on.

Tennyson swallowed hard and, between sniffles, began to explain what had happened. "I was just touching the table with my foot," she whimpered, "and the lady told me to stop. I did, right away, Aunt Elinor. Then I put my hands on the top of the table, and the lady came back and told me not to touch it. She was really being mean. Then she pushed my chair. . . ."

Elinor's stomach lurched. She had been intently watching the young girl in her charge, and no one had come up to the child, much less spoken or moved the chair. Elinor questioned the child's story but gave Tennyson a hug, saying softly, "I told you not to touch the antiques." Then she grabbed the boys' hands and headed to the Rib Room for brunch. Braden and Kingston piped up, almost in unison, "The lady was mean to us, too!" Elinor felt her knees go weak. . . .

In 1788, on Good Friday, the Catholic day of mourning just before Easter, a devastating fire ravaged the small, struggling Creole city cradled in the crescent-shaped bend of the mighty Mississippi River. The house of Don Narciso Alva was completely destroyed, and the two lots on which it sat were sold to Don Juan Paillet a few months later. Spain, in control of New Orleans since 1762, insisted that when vulnerable French wooden cottages and town houses fell victim to extreme weather, rot, hurricanes, or fire, new structures of brick masonry would rise from the rubble. On his newly purchased real estate, Paillet built a sizable house on the larger plot and a smaller one on the adjoining lot; both would remain in his family's possession until 1878. The main

Spanish Colonial town house was leased to Pierre Maspero, who opened La Bourse de Maspero or "Maspero's Exchange," as it was known by the American merchants pouring into the city after the Louisiana Purchase. Maspero's coffeehouse was the best-known slave auction mart in the city, as well as a meeting place where prominent businessmen discussed trade and politics. Town criers announced the sensational news of the day to those assembled in the coffeehouse. Pirates Jean and Pierre Lafitte used the second floor for secret meetings with "respectable" men who came to see them privately about smuggled booty. Downstairs, New Orleans's first Chamber of Commerce was organized in 1806. For many years mail was distributed at the exchange, and journalists and editors lorded over their special corner discussing the news of the day and literary and civic achievements.

In 1814, designating Maspero's as the headquarters, the citizens of New Orleans formed the Committee of Public Safety to organize opposition against the invading British army and awaited Andrew Jackson's command. It is said that Jackson also met with Jean Lafitte behind the batten, vertical board, shuttered doors of Maspero's second floor to solicit the services of the "Buccaneers of Barataria" for the war effort.

"And on my left, the slave exchange," carriage drivers called out as they passed by Maspero's, where terrified human beings, fresh off slave ships, sweltered in the exchange's entresol level, the hidden storage room with a low ceiling. Tucked between the first-floor commercial space and the expansive rooms above, the cramped area could only be accessed through the ceiling door of the bottom floor. The lingering spirits of those sold to the highest bidder, cruel or merciful, abound here.

In the 1830s the property was sold to James Hewlett, who changed the name to Hewlett's Exchange. Real estate auctions were held in three languages: English, French, and Spanish. On Saturdays the exchange still held the popular slave auctions. Private clubs were part of the Creole lifestyle, and the second-floor rooms of the exchange were reserved for gambling and billiards. Hewlett's was so successful that plans were made for a bigger and better establishment, to be called the City Exchange. This new structure would cover the entire block and include a lavish hotel. Hewlett commissioned architect Jacques Nicolas Bussiere de Pouilly to build a Creole palace on his French Quarter property, reminiscent of the flamboyant edifices along the Rue de Rivoli in Paris. The new City Exchange coffeehouse was successful under Hewlett's management. Land and slave auctions continued, and wealthy businessmen enjoyed an opulent place to dine, trade, buy and sell, even entertain their mistresses. When the three-story St. Louis Exchange Hotel opened, it annexed the coffeehouse, and the slave auctions were moved to the hotel's spacious rotunda. The hotel had a Spanish cook who invented the now world-famous Creole thickened soup, gumbo. The St. Louis was the first to serve soup, meat pies, and oyster patties to guests at the bar during lunchtime, free of charge. Other establishments in the area imitated this popular custom.

Fire destroyed the St. Louis Hotel in the early 1840s, but it was quickly rebuilt using de Pouilly's original plans. The building was further enlarged, and the name was changed to the Hotel Royal. Known for its architectural splendor, the ballroom hosted lavish Mardi Gras balls and social celebrations for the next twenty years. The Civil War, or "the War of Northern Aggression" as the people of New Orleans called it,

brought an abrupt halt to the gaiety of city life. With Yankee warships anchored off the bank of the Mississippi River,
New Orleans reluctantly surrendered. The Hotel Royal took
on a new role as a military hospital, and it remained as such
until the end of the war. During the severe Reconstruction
years, the hotel passed through several hands and again
entered the history books for housing the infamous Carpet-
bagger Legislature and serving as the state capitol before it
moved to Baton Rouge in 1882.

Two years later, the building was again a hotel, but less
than eight years later, it was abandoned, and its marble walls,
melancholy reminders of bygone glory days, were left to dete-
riorate. During the bubonic plague of 1914, the dilapidated
structure was condemned as rat-infested. The building was
torn down after the 1915 hurricane inflicted still further devastation. It remained a vacant lot for years until the Hotel
Corporation of America offered to invest in the property, on
one condition—it wanted to build a very big hotel. Architects
were asked to draw plans conforming to new preservation
laws imposed by the Vieux Carré Commission. The final structure used the stone arches of the original St. Louis Hotel, and
its Spanish wrought ironwork was meticulously replicated.
Specially designed upper windows made the hotel fit in with
neighboring buildings, and a rooftop garden and pool were
added. Called the Royal Orleans when it opened in 1960, the
hotel was a success from the outset. Now the Omni Royal
Orleans, the hotel is once again "the" place for past and present celebrities, from Luciano Pavarotti, Muhammad Ali, and
Jane Fonda to Richard Nixon, Patti LaBelle, and Paul Newman.
Even Lassie rested her head here.

The hotel is said to be haunted. From the prosperous Creole days through the austere Civil War aftermath, numerous

spirits have hung around. Hotel guests have reported seeing animated faces in the paintings that adorn the walls of the hotel. These ghostly visages are not part of the paintings but appear and disappear as if trying to be part of the grand activities. The faces of ghosts also pop up in photos taken in the hotel.

A maid who died at the hotel still checks up on her guests on the second floor. Since the hotel had no heat during her tenure, part of this maid's duties included heating the guests' beds by putting a bedwarmer, a copper-bottom pan filled with coals, at the foot of the bed and tucking the covers in all around the bed to keep in the warmth. Modern-day guests report waking up with the bed-sheets tucked snugly around them. She is ever vigilant to the needs of her guests. She turns on faucets to run baths as evening creeps in and then forgets to turn off the water as she hurries off to check on another guest. She also turns lights on and off and flushes toilets while she cleans in the middle of the night.

The hotel is decorated with nineteenth-century antiques, and paranormal investigators think as many as fifty ghosts are connected to the hotel. Because of strong attachments to their belongings in a previous life, the owners' spirits stay on to watch over their beloved possessions. They often play pranks on guests who make unseemly comments about the antiques and admonish those who abuse them. Other ghosts like to lock doors, especially in a suite whose number is kept secret so as not to scare off potential paying patrons. Front desk managers know that if they get a desperate call from this room, they will have some explaining to do. In room 227, guests have often been scared off by the constant phone ringing. When they answer, no one is on the other end. It's a common occurrence, and the night manager can't explain it. Paranormal energy abounds here; the area where slaves were auctioned is now a loading dock. Physical manifestations and cold spots have been detected. Guests complain that ghostly beings follow them around as they pass through the lobby, eat in the dining room, or pace the pavement outside waiting for a friend.

Elinor slowly lowered herself back on the overstuffed chair. The room was spinning, the furnishings had come alive, and faces were staring at her from the paintings on the walls. She fumbled in her purse for a tissue, took a deep breath, and looked around the lobby. The children were cool and collected. "I'm hungry," said Tennyson, now fully recovered from her fall off the chair. The boys were pulling her arm toward the dining room, "Let's go eat," they chimed. Elinor shook her head, squinted her eyes shut, and then opened them wide. The bronze statues and crystal chandeliers seemed settled once again in the elegant lobby. The furnishings were in their proper places and the paintings on the walls were quiet, but she wondered what strange stories they could tell. Elinor stood up, her undaunted New Orleans spirit at the ready. "Okay, kids, let's go eat. Who wants eggs Benedict, and who wants to tell me all about the mean lady?"

Chapter 4
Bourbon Orleans Gala

The historic Bourbon Orleans at 717 Rue Orleans between Royal and Bourbon Streets has a long and colorful past. Today it is one of the city's most beloved landmarks, synonymous with culture and good taste. Brides-to-be book their wedding receptions far in advance, knowing many guests will eagerly accept their invitation to celebrate at the Bourbon Orleans. The hotel stands in the heart of the French Quarter, and locals look forward to the festivities held there throughout the year, from Mardi Gras balls and the scrumptious Mother's Day Champagne Brunch to the Living History Christmas pageant that includes visits from New Orleans historical figures such as Baroness Pontalba, Marie Laveau, John James Audubon, Jean Lafitte, and Papa Noel dressed in period clothing. For a party-loving, fine food-appreciating, and convivial metropolis, the Bourbon Orleans is king, and lingering spirits will make sure a good time is had by all.

Kristen got out of the taxi and entered the Bourbon Orleans hotel. The trip from the airport had been a rush-hour nightmare, and now the Old World charm and opulent French decor of the tranquil lobby were welcomed relief. She was in the Crescent City because cousin Aiden was getting married. The wedding would be at the St. Louis Cathedral, and the large reception would be in the Bourbon Orleans. Kristen had moved away from New Orleans, where she had grown up in a big French family. Even after her divorce, she had not returned.

Jack was also attending the wedding, only because he felt obligated. He planned to sit in the back of the church during the ceremony, say a quick "Congratulations" to his friend at the reception, and head home.

Kristen arrived at the ballroom ahead of the wedding party and waited for the bride and groom to appear. The music was playing, but she felt drawn to the windows, where a young woman stood looking out across the courtyard. She walked over and saw that the woman was nearly in tears. "Can I help you?" Kristen asked. The woman said, "I can't find him. He said he would be here, but . . ."

Jack had crept out of the cathedral and strolled around Jackson Square to give the bride and groom plenty of time to greet their guests before his quick "hello and have a happy life." When he peeked into the ballroom, the couple was busy taking pictures, so he hung around the reception area talking to a man dressed in a military uniform who asked him where "she" was. Jack thought it strange that someone would be dressed in costume so early in the day. But, hey, this was New Orleans. . . .

In the early 1800s New Orleans was still reeling from being tossed around among countries. France had ceded the area to Spain, only to take it back again. Then in 1803, France sold the Louisiana territory to the United States, a country, in the eyes of the French aristocrats, of savages and backwoods ruffians. The citizens resented the influx of Anglo-Americans and tightened their hold on French customs and language. In fact when William C. C. Claiborne, appointed territorial governor, spoke from the balcony of the Cabildo to the assembled citizens for the first time, most could not understand a word he said, since they did not speak English. The Americans learned quickly they were not welcome in French society, and most didn't understand the customs in any case.

Parisian John Davis had escaped the uprising in Saint-Domingue (now Haiti) and made his way to New Orleans, a city so comfortable to his nature, he decided to stay. In 1817, he opened the Orleans Ballroom, a richly decorated place to host the city's most select affairs. Lavish carnival balls and masquerade galas were held here by and for the city's elite. The ballroom was resplendent with the finest luxuries of the day, from lofty ceilings with sparkling chandeliers to mirror-polished floors. The windows of the second-floor ballroom looked out over Orleans Street, and the back of the Church of St. Louis, beyond the lush courtyard below, could be seen from its balconies.

But the Orleans Ballroom served another, more integral function in New Orleans society. It was the setting for the famous Quadroon Balls, evening socials during which beautiful fair-skinned quadroon and octoroon women, one-fourth to one-eighth African, anticipated selection as mistresses of wealthy Creole gentlemen. Mixed-race couples were forbidden to marry, but the mistresses were ensured financial support by white gentry through the system of plaçage. A ticket to a Quadroon Ball cost two dollars, ensuring that only white men of a certain social rank could attend. Music and liquor flowed so lavishly in this opulent setting, it was said that the capitals of Europe were envious. The Orleans Ballroom hosted many of the city's most prestigious social and historical events. Elegant masked balls, the forerunner of today's Carnival celebration, were held there as early as

1823. In 1825, a grand ball was held to honor the Marquis de Lafayette, of Revolutionary War fame. In 1827, the Orleans Ballroom became a legislative meeting place where, it is said, Andrew Jackson announced he was running for president of the United States.

The first Théâtre d'Orléans, constructed in 1815, had burned down soon after opening, and impresario Davis saw this as his opportunity to rebuild the theater on property adjacent to his popular ballroom. Davis was the first to bring grand French opera to his adopted city, and the Théâtre d'Orléans reigned supreme in the operatic world prior to the Civil War. Quite fittingly, the opening performance was dedicated to Davis, who had put so much effort into making the production a worthy spectacle. Davis booked singers, musicians, and actors from Europe and beyond to entertain New Orleanians during opera and theater seasons. The works of Gioachino Rossini, Daniel François Esprit Auber, and other popular composers were highlighted. Four Rossini operas, *La Gazza Ladra*, *La Donna del Lago*, *Le Comte Ory*, and *L'Italiana in Algeri*, celebrated their United States premieres at the Théâtre d'Orléans. A February 28, 1828, poster marked the performance of *The Vestal*, a grand opera in three acts, and a vaudeville skit, "Monsieur Jovial" or "Singing Constable." Davis continued serving the city's cultural scene by adding exclusive dining and gaming rooms to his hotel-ballroom-theater complex. Davis and his son, Pierre, continued as managers of the Orleans Ballroom and the Théâtre d'Orléans until 1859.

The Civil War halted the city's unfettered nightlife. The theater—with its galleries, two tiers of box seats, some latticed so those in mourning could attend unseen, balcony, and exclusive supper rooms that entertained more than

1,300 theatergoers a night—burned down in 1866. The ballroom was saved, and the Innocenti, a paramilitary Sicilian political club, held its meetings in the ballroom to plan for the 1868 presidential election. Soon after that the ballroom served as the First District Court.

In 1881, the site was acquired by the Sisters of the Holy Family, an early order of African-American nuns. The ballroom and adjacent theater property now housed a convent, an orphanage for *enfants de couleur*, and St. Mary's Academy for African-American girls. History records that many orphans died of yellow fever in the medical ward set up to treat the children. In the 1960s the sisters moved to a new convent and school, and the Bourbon Orleans Hotel took over the site. The original Orleans Ballroom became the heart of the hotel and a reminder to visitors of a vibrant past.

Most memories attached to the Orleans Ballroom and the buildings of the Bourbon Orleans Hotel are good ones; perhaps that is why so many spirits have remained behind. More than seventeen ghosts, most of which are small children, have been reported.

The most common haunting is that of a young girl who roams the ballroom stopping to gaze silently out the window and the specter of a Confederate soldier in the reception hall outside the ballroom. The story is this: A man met his lover here for one last evening together. He told her he must depart in the morning to fight in the war. He promised to return, meet here, and marry her. Unfortunately the soldier died. The devastated young woman took her own life. The couple still search for each other; she roams the ballroom and her fiancé in a Confederate uniform paces the reception area outside the ballroom. Guests and staff see the couple several times a year.

The spirit of a dashing Creole gentleman also resides in the ballroom. He is quite the ladies' man, and young women, turning around to see who is kissing their necks and caressing their cheeks, see a fleeing apparition. The hotel has many friendly, but mischievous, resident ghosts. The fifth floor is home to a little fair-haired girl who rolls her ball down the hall, then chases it through walls, and on the sixth floor guests complain of television sets turning on and off, channels changing inexplicably, and running water in bathroom sinks and showers. A banquet server setting up for a private reception reported that the drinking glasses were rearranged when she turned her back and then she heard children giggling. Others have reported unexplained disturbed linens and tipped glasses, as if children at play had bumped the serving tables. Guests complain that, when they press the button for the main floor, the elevator takes them to the sixth floor (where the convent's children's infirmary had been located) but no one is there when the door opens.

There are sad spirits here as well. Guests report children crying in the halls; perhaps these are the yellow fever orphans. The seventh floor is home to an aging Confederate soldier who parades up and down the hallways with his rifle thrown over his shoulder. Before the modern restoration, the hotel restrooms had been gaming rooms, and it seems a dejected gambler still lingers. It was here that a young gambler, losing not only the hand, but the deed to his home, put a pistol in his mouth and pulled the trigger. This sad, distraught, and, indeed, unlucky spirit dressed in old-fashioned formal clothes is often spotted around the mirrors.

Spirits of the holy nuns also reside in the hotel. A chef working in the second-floor kitchen knocked two pans off a table and then cursed loudly. The lights inexplicably went out, and he was mysteriously slapped across the face. When the lights came back on, the man rushed to the closest mirror. He found a vivid red hand print on his face. A construction worker reported that when he inadvertently hurt himself and uttered a vulgarity, an unseen hand slapped him across the face. A room-service employee says that when she was putting towels in a guest bathroom, she looked into the mirror and saw a nun's image reflected there. She felt a rush of air at her back, and when she turned around, the holy sister was staring right at her. She opened her eyes wide with disbelief, and then the nun turned and walked away. Her supervisor told her not to worry, that the woman had been haunting the room for quite some time.

A pirate specter named Raoul smiles at women as they enter the ballroom. Legend has it that he was killed in a duel over a woman's honor. He's not sorry he accepted the challenge, since he was after all a true Southern gentleman. His laughter is often heard across the ballroom as his spirit appears, then vanishes. In the lobby of the hotel, guests and staff have reported smelling tobacco smoke just before spotting an elderly man with a newspaper and a large cigar. When they stare in his direction, he raises an annoyed eyebrow, folds his newspaper roughly, stands up, and brazenly disappears.

The forlorn woman, tears in her eyes, took Kristen by the hand and led her around the ballroom, desperately seeking the unknown "he." Kristen was just about to leave the poor soul to her quest when the woman pulled her toward the entrance door. Meanwhile, Jack was trying to distance himself from the strange, costumed man and, in fact, had thought about skipping the reception altogether. When his odd friend began to move toward the stairs with him, Jack was determined to get away. He turned around to go back toward the ballroom, where he knew only invited guests would be granted entry. He stopped dead in his tracks, mouth open. Who was coming out of the ballroom, but Kristen Michelle, his high school sweetheart and the only woman he had ever truly loved. They had lost contact years ago. . . . He wondered if she was still married. He turned to make sure he had successfully shaken off the oddball who had befriended him; thankfully he was gone. Kristen felt the woman who had steered her toward the reception area softly release her hand, and when she turned, the woman had disappeared. Kristen gave Jack a big hug. "Fancy meeting you here," she said. Jack smiled unabashedly, thinking how the most important moment of his life almost didn't happen at all.

Chapter 5

The Dauphine
Orleans Madame

The Dauphine Orleans Hotel completed a total renovation of guest rooms and public spaces in 2008. It is common for ghost sightings to escalate when renovations take place, and this hotel has its stories. The Dauphine offers "boutique hotel" guest rooms in structures that are nearly as old as the city herself. Not only do the owners admit that apparitions have been sighted on the premises, they are happy to discuss the behavior of the ghostly visitors. A staff member once said, "We will continue to investigate the paranormal phenomena recorded at the Dauphine Orleans in the hopes to unveil more psychic echoes from the past, particularly our former female residents." The hotel is a gem, deep in the heart of the French Quarter, with patio rooms, separate cottages, three secluded courtyards, and, oh, yes, ethereal visitors from the bygone days of old New Orleans.

Mari and Patty were freelance writers and amateur ghost hunters. They were part of a group that followed up on reports, submitted to its website, of recent paranormal activity in various locations across the country. This time a lead had come about a possible haunting in their own backyard, New Orleans. The women were eager to get going and rechecked that they had everything they needed for the night they would spend at the Dauphine Orleans, a hotel in the middle of the French Quarter, reputedly the most haunted area in the country. They checked in at the front desk in late afternoon and then went to their room to unpack their equipment and take a short nap. When night was well under way and some of the dinner crowd had dispersed from the sundry restaurants and the narrow, noise-echoing streets of the area, it was time for the ghost hunters to begin their stakeout.

Mari and Patty took the elevator down to the main lobby of the hotel and walked silently toward one of the lush courtyards to set up a digital video recorder. They also set one up near the patio rooms, some of the hotel's oldest structures. An hour or so later, they were ready to check out the hotel's cottages across the street, where John James Audubon had painted his birds and where Civil War soldiers had reportedly spent time convalescing from war wounds. The Audubon cottage was unoccupied this night, and the women had persuaded the night manager to give them access to the room for a short while. They took out their K2 meters, handheld electromagnetic field detectors used to track energy sources by recording spikes on a grid. Because spirits are entities of energy, it is believed that their energy can disturb the electromagnetic field when they are trying to contact someone or take on a bodily shape. A cold spot is often reported in places where ghosts are said to appear because spirits absorb the energy around them in order to manifest either physically or vocally. Mari was the first to report some eerie feelings, especially near the back wall and bathroom. The women were discussing the history of soldiers who had passed this way and the various manifestations guests had reported, when Patty suddenly gave a start. She looked down—the K2 meter was spiking at regular intervals. . . .

By the early 1800s, commerce ruled the day in New Orleans. Cotton was king, and wealthy magnates were buying up modest properties in the French Quarter and building lavish mansions. One such merchant was Samuel Hermann, a Jewish immigrant from Roedelheim, Germany. Upon his arrival in Louisiana, he settled in an area called German Coast, a German enclave since the 1720s in St. John the Baptist Parish, northwest of New Orleans, and the site, in 1811, of the largest slave insurrection in US history, known as the German Coast Uprising. Here Hermann met Creole Catholic Marie Emeranthe Becnel Brou, married her, and began his career as a successful entrepreneur. He moved downriver to New Orleans in 1816 and a few years later acquired a substantial amount of property on St. Louis Street in the French Quarter. He settled his family into a large, older home on the estate and amassed substantial wealth through cotton brokering and banking. He had three sons, Samuel Jr., Florian, and Lucien, who followed in his footsteps in the banking industry. His daughter, Marie Virginie, was educated as a day student at the Ursuline Convent and at the age of sixteen made her debut, a joyous occasion preserved in a portrait by Jean Joseph Vaudechamp that has survived to this day.

While Hermann's family life flourished, his commercial empire also grew in importance, and he made plans to erect a palatial town house that would reflect his wealth on the home front and his stature in the business world. In 1831, he demolished the family's homestead and built a mansion that included a large, spacious house, outdoor kitchens, an enclosed courtyard, a horse stable, and other outbuildings. Hermann contracted with architect and builder William Brand to draw up plans in the Federal style of homes being built in Philadelphia and Boston. Brand insisted, however, on keeping some iconic Creole features, like the enclosed courtyard. Hermann was demanding, calling for only the best "brick, sand, and cypress" to be used in the construction. He was also a precise man who included in the building contract minute details such as the size of the nails to be used and the number of coats of paint. The brick-walled home was magnificent, with a fitting exterior for the beautiful stone fireplaces and pecky cypress and pine beams inside.

This "Golden Age" was enjoyed by Hermann and men like him. The wharves on the riverfront were busy with trade and commerce. The wealth of the country was carried on the river, the plantation system was at its peak, the city was enjoying immense prosperity, and extravagant balls were held nearly every night. There was a movement from the center of the city to areas outside the French Quarter, uptown mansions were springing up, and Garden District homes were the rage. Theaters and opera flourished as did gambling houses and bordellos. Unfortunately Hermann found himself a victim of the national financial panic of 1837, reportedly losing two million dollars. He sold off his French Quarter home in 1844 to Judge Felix Grima, a graduate of the College d'Orleans, a city university in the Faubourg Tremé area of New Orleans that emphasized the classics. Grima studied law with Etienne Mazureau, a distinguished attorney. Grima was a Criminal Court judge for a few years and used one of the spacious first-floor rooms as his library and office. When his teacher and mentor, Mazareau, was appointed state attorney general, he made Grima his assistant.

The rise of the railroad as a competitor to river traffic added to the woes of New Orleans and foreshadowed the end of the Golden Age of steamboats. The French Quarter was in a state of flux as wealthy residents moved to more spacious areas, leaving the narrow cobblestone streets and alleys to commercial enterprises. May Baily's popular bordello, licensed in 1857 and just down the street from where Hermann had built his private residence, signaled the change that was happening. By the mid-1860s New Orleans was occupied by Federal troops. The remaining small Creole cottages along Dauphine Street housed soldiers during and after the war.

Ownership of the buildings that were ultimately to become a landmark French Quarter hotel changed hands more than twenty times. The main structure of the Hermann House has been preserved as the Hermann-Grima Museum, but some of the structures originally part of the Samuel Hermann estate, including the Hermann House Courtyard guest rooms and the rooms and suites of the Carriage House that overlook the lush courtyard, were purchased to be renovated as the Dauphine Orleans Hotel, which opened in 1969, displaying the Creole extravagance of the period from 1830 to 1860. The humble cottage where John James Audubon had kept a studio and painted his famous "Birds of America" series at 550 Dauphine Street is today the hotel's main meeting room. Some cottages that once housed Civil War soldiers are also part of the hotel, and guests report sightings of soldiers in the courtyard and swimming pool area (the pool is believed be the oldest in the French Quarter). A man with dark hair, dressed in a military uniform, is often seen in the courtyard.

Renovation work on the main hotel building brought the ghosts out of the woodwork. Guests talk about the unknown woman who dances across the courtyard. She is so light on her feet and so quick that guests can catch only fleeting glimpses of her. Hotel patrons staying in the patio rooms report footsteps and running overhead as well as the bouncing and shaking of beds in the early hours of the morning and late in the afternoon. When staff members go upstairs to check the disturbances, the room is empty. An impish specter resides here, too. No one has ever seen the sprite that likes to lock empty rooms from the inside. Many guests report the feeling of being watched.

A ghost, seen so often that the staff refers to him as "George," reportedly haunts the hotel. Suites 110 and 111 are known for weird occurrences. Several haunted tales describe knocks on doors and ghostly moans emanating from these rooms. Others report heavy objects moving about at odd times. Ghost hunters have staked out these suites and have detected a temperature drop and electromagnetic activity in the back of the room near the closet.

Recently a front desk clerk told the story of a guest who complained of an old man who had mysteriously entered their locked room to ask if everything was all right. When he was shown out the door, the guest looked down the hallway and saw no one. The man had simply vanished into thin air. The clerk says such paranormal activity is quite frequent. Maintenance workers report seeing an unknown black man in his mid-fifties in the area of the Carriage House and often report that shadows seem to follow them around supervising their duties.

Today many ghostly appearances are reported in the bar, aptly called May Baily's. It seems young, sleek specters are still seeking generous patrons to wine and dine them. These ghostly inhabitants appear as well-dressed "ladies of the evening" who wander, unchecked, throughout the bar, dancing and swaying to silent musical beats. One determined young woman constantly rearranges the liquor bottles behind the bar. It seems she has her own sorting system and gets annoyed when the bartenders don't follow it. Pictures of some of the ladies, a few of the local gossip pages from the 1900s, and the actual license of May Baily's bordello adorn the wall. A red light burns nearby in the courtyard, reminiscent of the wild, rumpus days of the "bordello" guest rooms just above the bar, which are still used today as part of the hotel.

The oldest ghost story is of a young couple brutally tortured and murdered by pirates in the 1700s in one of the early-built structures. It seems the spirits of the young people have remained, despite rebuilding and extensive refurbishing. Today cherrywood armoires and bronze chandeliers evoke a past glory in which guests and spirits can dream on goose down pillows and sip libations at high tea served every afternoon.

By the time Mari and Patty made their way over to May Baily's bar, it was after midnight. There didn't seem to be too much activity, until a group of attractive young men entered the bar. Perhaps it was a bachelor party having a grand time, but in any case they were vivacious and noisy. Suddenly electromagnetic field spikes were detected on Patty's K2. Patty whispered to her friend that these exuberant thirty-somethings must have excited the spirits of the resident ladies of the night. K2 devices allow communication with ghosts in a way. Researchers can ask questions, and ghosts can stir the energy around them, creating fluctuations in the electromagnetic field readings that can be recorded. In hushed tones, Patty explained to the female spirits that she had a few questions. To answer the question, she directed the spirits to disturb the energy around the meter. One spike meant "yes," while two spikes in rapid succession meant "no." It was time to ask some questions. Patty cleared her throat, "Were you one of May Baily's girls?" The screen lit up. . . .

Chapter 6
Old Soldiers
Stay the Course

The Beauregard-Keyes House stands as a testament to all that was grand during the heyday of New Orleans, an age that was to end abruptly as the Civil War claimed its victims. The home's unconventional architecture exhibits the transition between the receding early 1800s Creole and the emerging American styles. This house, on the National Register of Historic Places and full of period antiques and portraits of Beauregard, has been home to not one, but three, well-known personalities: General Pierre Gustave Toutant Beauregard, known as the "Creole Napoleon"; Paul Morphy, who stunned the world with his chess-playing expertise; and Frances Parkinson Keyes, the novelist who preserved forever the splendor of the Crescent City in her novels. Many spirits are also in residence here; in fact, the Beauregard-Keyes House is considered one of the most haunted sites in New Orleans and is referred to as a "ghost dormitory" by Victor C. Klein in "New Orleans Ghosts."

Annamarie put her hand to the official plaque that proclaimed 1113 Chartres Street as the residence of General P. G. T. Beauregard, CSA, 1868. Then she climbed the curved side granite staircase to the first-floor gallery, passing her hand ever so slightly over the beautiful wrought-iron banister. She stood erect at the wood-paneled double door to the spacious Beauregard-Keyes House, straightened her full antebellum skirt, smoothed her long, silky sleeves, and snuggled her feet further into the blue satin slippers. Then she quickly glanced across the street at the Old Ursuline Convent, made the sign of the cross, and took an extra deep breath.

Today was her first day as a guide, and she was very nervous. Ready to welcome today's tourists, she tried to put last evening's bizarre occurrences out of her mind. The night had started well enough. She had walked the short distance from her French Quarter apartment and arrived at the Beauregard-Keyes House, where she and the other novice guides were given one last briefing, costume check, and name badges. Refreshments had been offered, but Annamarie was way too nervous to eat or drink. While the others were socializing, she decided to review her history of the house one more time. Wanting to practice out loud and alone, she returned to one of the empty rooms and pretended a group of tourists was in front of her as she pointed to a painting. It was getting late, and she was feeling weary from the anxiety and tension of the next day's task.

She sat down against the wall, put her head back, and closed her eyes. What seemed like seconds passed, and when she opened her eyes, the room was in total darkness. Where was everyone? She felt her way to the door and looked down the hall toward the ballroom, where an eerie light drew her mysteriously to the room. When she peered in, she felt her heart jump from her chest to her throat. The scene before her was most certainly otherworldly, and though she wanted to run away, she couldn't. Frozen to the spot, she had no choice but to stare at the horror swirling before her eyes.

The Ursuline nuns originally owned the property on which the Beauregard-Keyes House stands. In 1825 they sold four lots to auctioneer Joseph Le Carpentier. The Beauregard-Keyes House, sometimes referred to as Le Carpentier-Beauregard-Keyes House, was designed by François Correjolles using Greek Revival and Colonial-era features; it was built by James Lambert in 1826. It has been said that Le Carpentier made his wealth by selling, at public auctions, the goods acquired by pirate Jean Lafitte. He was also the grandfather of Paul Morphy, who would become one of the most famous chess players in the world. Young Paul was born in this house in 1837. Unlike most houses at the time with inner courtyards, the Beauregard-Keyes House was unique in having side gardens that sat in full view of the public at the corner of Chartres and Ursuline Streets.

There is some mixed history here, but one story goes that as an ambitious major hailed for his service during the Mexican-American War, Pierre Gustave Toutant Beauregard moved into the Chartres Street house with his wife, Caroline Deslonde, in 1860. His fifteen-year military service was rewarded with an appointment as commandant of West Point. Beauregard left New Orleans to assume his command on the eve of Louisiana's secession from the Union on January 26, 1861. As a patriotic Southerner, he was relieved of his duties after serving only five days as commandant. Jefferson Davis, president of the Confederacy, had his own plans for Beauregard and called him to the South's new capital in Montgomery, Alabama. Beauregard was sent to South Carolina and gave the order to fire on Fort Sumter, the action that officially started the Civil War. He became one of the most famous Confederate leaders with many victories, including the First Battle of Bull Run, but there was one most regrettable loss at Shiloh. General Beauregard returned to his house in New Orleans when the war ended, but it was not a happy homecoming. His beloved Caroline had died a year earlier, and he was in financial trouble. In 1866 he stood on the granite steps of his Chartres Street home and spoke to a crowd of men, some still in tattered uniforms. As a native son, he was cheered and hailed as a hero. However, it seems Beauregard could not shake the memories of his devastating loss at the Battle of Shiloh. There were rumors of his roaming the halls at night calling Caroline's name, donning his uniform, and attacking an invisible enemy. Friends reported that he spent hours pacing the dining room in the middle of the night, and his emotional rantings were loud enough for the neighbors to hear. Beauregard would never recover from his memories of soldiers wounded and dying on the bloody battlefield. His fortunes eventually ran out and he vacated his beautiful French Quarter home. Stories of ghostly happenings in the General's prior home began in 1893, the year the general died. People passing by his former residence claimed to hear a tired, lamenting, old voice repeating one word over and over again: Shiloh. Sometimes in the middle of the night, the shadowy figure of General Beauregard in his Confederate uniform appears in the ballroom. His appearance is always accompanied by a freezing drop in temperature. Soon the ballroom is transformed into a bloody battlefield, a ghostly Shiloh where bodies are slaughtered and torn apart by gunshot. Witnesses (yes, witnesses . . . owners, neighbors, passersby, managers of the historic house, tour guides, ghost hunters) say the scene is drenched in a nightmare quality as if it were a phantom reenactment. Weary soldiers stand in rows, deathly still while drums beat and bugles call. Rifle and musket shots suddenly ring out, and men begin to fall; shot in the arm, the leg, the chest, they crumble to the floor. As the soldiers fall, their bloody flesh and skin disappear leaving bare skull and bones in a weird dreamscape. Many cogitate that the mutilated and mangled specters are not the dead ghosts of the fallen men at Shiloh—after all the battle took place in Tennessee—but rather the hellish ghosts of Beauregard's nightmares reenacting the destruction and death that tortured him nightly.

Though some New Orleanians tried to preserve the stately Beauregard house, their actions were thwarted by the numerous stories of war reenactments, musket fire, battle cries, and wounded soldiers moaning through the night. Fears of ghosts and eerie occurrences on the property prevented civic renovation ideas from becoming reality. By the early 1900s the house had passed into the ownership of the Giacona family, who added an exotic flavor to the old house. The aroma of olive oil and garlic wafted from the kitchen, and colorful clothing hung to dry in the noonday sun. It is here that we meet a second group of spirits vying for haunting privileges. The Giaconas were making a fortune as wine merchants. During those raw and rough times of the early twentieth century, powerful immigrant groups ruled the underbelly of New Orleans. The Italian mafia, hard-hearted and ruthless, demanded protection money from the Giaconas, who refused to pay, thinking they could protect themselves well enough. When the Giaconas became a hit target of the Sicilian mafia, the family took proactive measures to turn the Beauregard house into a fortress. Windows were barred, doors double-bolted, and family members heavily armed. One night in 1909, as the Giaconas were seated at their elegant dinner table, movement was detected in the gallery. Handguns exploded, and four dark figures responded in kind. Bone-splintering cries rang out as blood spewed the walls. When the carnage had ceased, three mafia thugs lay dead, gushing blood running over the balcony floorboards to the ground below. Screams could be heard as a fourth man disappeared into the dark cover of night. Local newspapers reported the gun battle, making note of the large number of bullets found in the bodies. Commander Thomas Capo of the Third Precinct Station arrived about 2:45 a.m. and described the scene as "covered with blood." The Giaconas were vindicated of murder charges, remained in the home for a few more years, and then disappeared. Some say gruesome screams can still be heard from the house, ringing out in the dead of night. The house changed hands several times, slowing sinking into ruin.

In 1925, the property changed hands again. The new owner announced that he would erect a macaroni factory on the lot. A group of enthusiastic women formed the Beauregard Memorial Association and raised enough funds to save General Beauregard's house, even though most of the gardens were demolished when the factory was built.

The ghosts in this house are unique. They do not interact with those who hear and see them, although for years neighbors have reported battle noises, musket fire, and the clash of sabers. Others have heard men shout curses and seen trails of blood flowing from the upstairs gallery. Passersby have been startled by guns waving in the air by unseen hands or wounded figures flying from the porch. Don't think the police will respond to your calls about strange noises or gunshots at 1113 Chartres, because they won't.

In 1944, the well-known novelist Frances Parkinson Keyes rented the house and eventually acquired it and the corner property (the macaroni factory). While working on several of her books here, *Dinner at Antoine's, Chess Player,* and *Blue Camellia,* Keyes began her own restoration efforts to bring the house and gardens back to their former glory. She began the Keyes Foundation, which owns the home today. Lovely magnolias, sculpted boxwoods, and an iron fountain adorn the brick-walled garden duplicating the original design by Anais Philippon Merle, the wife of New Orleans Swiss consul John A. Merle who in the 1860s and 1870s planted a formal garden and enclosed it with brick walls with grill windows so passersby could peer in at the garden. It is maintained by the Garden Study Club of New Orleans. Keyes died in July 1970 in the Beauregard House.

Ghosts from this era include Keyes's beloved cocker spaniel, Lucky, who died just a few days after his mistress. It seems he still roams the premises. The house director has reported seeing a "ghost cat" called Caroline who wears a soundless bell around her neck and rubs up against tourists. No one knows who she is or whom the cat belonged to.

Docents in period costume welcome visitors to the historic Beauregard-Keyes House, and Keyes's collection of antique dolls, teapots, fans, and fascinating folk costumes are on exhibit. A Tea Party for the Dolls is an annual children's event.

Annamarie shook her head to clear her mind of the shadowy, sinister shapes of mangled men and slaughtered horses. When she had regained her wits and fled the house, she was surprised to learn how much time had passed. The house was empty and dark. Everyone had departed, not knowing she was embroiled in the unearthly carnage of a nightmarish battlefield. She could still smell the blood and decay. But today was a new day, and she had historical facts and figures to deliver to eager tourists. She put the phantoms behind her and welcomed in the first group. Smiling broadly, she quickly felt the terror rise against her chest. "I heard this house is haunted," said a gentleman in the rear of the group. "Have you ever seen a ghost here?" Her training had not prepared her for this: Should she tell them the truth . . . or not?

Chapter 7

The Lalaurie House of Death

The Lalaurie Mansion is said to be the most haunted of all the haunted houses in New Orleans. Its reputation is well deserved and well documented. Tourists look upon the Lalaurie Mansion and its story of inhumanity as a spine-tingling, perhaps overly dramatic tale. For locals, the mansion is the icon of terror, an anguished story told on dark, damp nights when fear and foreboding unite the city's past to the present. From the yellowed newsprint pages of nineteenth-century media to today's raconteurs, the epithet "the Haunted House" can only mean one place. Looming over its corner of the French Quarter, its bleak aura is reason enough for passersby to cross the street, purposefully avoiding the otherworldly life still active in the Lalaurie Mansion.

Karolyn and Mae, real estate colleagues in their company's Million-Dollar Club, would begin a new partnership today. Karolyn had a rich client interested in buying a house in the French Quarter, but her expertise was the uptown Garden District. She didn't want to lose her client to a more knowledgeable agent, so she had consulted Mae, who knew the Quarter inside and out. "My client wants a place in or near the French Quarter," Karolyn began. She was reluctant to say her client's name, but Mae read her colleague's mind. "Karolyn," she said, "let's be clear. I will not steal your client, no way, no how." Karolyn sighed, "Okay. It's Mary Aimee

Jacob." Karolyn continued, "You know, she's in that new sit-com about paranormal activity in New Orleans." "Oh, yeah. What's she looking for?" Mae asked. Karolyn began with the number of bedrooms and baths. Mae was concerned; French Quarter property was expensive. She interrupted, "How much does she want to spend?" Karolyn smiled. "Enough." "Well," Mae said, "I may have just the property for her."

Standing in front of the three-story edifice on Royal Street, Mae said, "You know it's haunted, right?" "No!" Karolyn said. "But this is getting interesting!" Mae unlocked the door. The women stood in the entryway, looking up, down, and around. "I thought you said the house was vacant?" Karolyn asked. "It is," Mae said. "Then who was that woman who just ran across the hallway with the little girl?" Karolyn was pointing to the top of the stairs. Mae, swallowing the lump in her throat, had not yet told Karolyn the ghostly details of the property. She guessed it was time to do so. "Well, Karolyn, I need to tell you about one of the previous owners of this house. . . ."

Brothers Jean and Henri Remairie built a Colonial home at 1140 Royal Street in the 1770s. The property then passed through several hands, including Edmond Soniat Dufossat and Barthélémy Louis de Macarty. By the 1830s, New Orleans was enjoying a prosperous period economically and culturally. The Civil War had not yet threatened the slave labor enabling wealthy citizens to enjoy this abundant life. Stories differ as to the early history of the property on the corner of Royal and Hospital (which became Governor Nicholls Street in 1911) Streets. Some say Macarty built a lavish mansion and then gave it to his daughter, Delphine; others say it was Delphine who had the home built. It is documented that by 1831 in an act of sale, preserved in the Notorial Archives of City Hall in New Orleans, the house was registered to "Madame Louis Lalaurie, neé Marie Delphine de Macarty." Delphine, by this time, had married her third husband, French physician Louis Lalaurie, and the couple moved into the house. Delphine was rich, beautiful, and cultured. She loved entertaining on a grand scale and served the finest food and rarest wines at lavish occasions.

Madame Lalaurie's many slaves made life easy for her. Rumors of her mistreatment of them surfaced; some say she enjoyed the good life at the expense of those who provided it for her. A neighbor reported seeing Delphine chasing one of her slave girls onto the roof of the house. The young girl held a hairbrush in her hands; Madame held a whip. The girl had snagged Delphine's long locks while brushing her hair and needed to be punished. Delphine chased the girl from the bedroom onto the rear gallery. The child took blow after blow, screaming and clinging to the balcony. Some said she jumped to her death to avoid further lashing, while others reported that the force of the blows caused the child to slip through the railing of the balcony. Regardless, the girl fell dead into the courtyard below. News reports said that neighbors had called out to Delphine, demanding she stop the assault. When things finally quieted, the neighbors went back to their nightly routines, but by the next day the authorities had been alerted as to what had happened. When the police came to the Lalaurie house to investigate, no body or even any evidence of a crime could be found. Madame Lalaurie denied the accusations. The investigation was closed, and life returned to normal for the Lalauries.

Ghostly stories started immediately. Neighbors reported cries and ear-piercing screams from the attic torture rooms. The subsequent history of the house has many versions. Here's one. The house was rebuilt to its former glory, with one notable change. The upper window from which the slave jumped to her death on the night of the fire was sealed shut. The first residents lasted only a short time, reporting ghostly slaves roaming the hallways, dragging cumbersome and clanging chains behind them. The tenants told tales of visiting children who claimed that a woman with a whip was chasing them.

In 1837 the mansion was bought by Pierre Edouard Trastour, who added a third floor and French Empire detailing. He sold the property to Charles Caffin. It was sold again in 1862 to the widow of Horace Cammack, a prosperous cotton merchant who had died yachting off the coast of Norway. Well-known architects Gallier and Esterbrook renovated the house in 1865 and 1866, according to their papers. The ghosts behaved themselves a little better during the property's next period as a school for girls, both black and white. By 1882 the building was turned into a music conservatory, which closed when the macabre rumors led to vacant seats at concerts.

From 1893 to 1916, Italian businessman Fortunato Greco ran a moderately successful bar on the lower floor of the mansion called the Haunted Saloon. He kept a record of his guests' descriptions of unearthly people and occurrences. In 1923, philanthropist William J. Warrington bought the house as a refuge for indigent men and boys. Though they were grateful for a roof over their heads, many complained about tormented spirits and agonized screams keeping them awake at night. Reports of attacks by "black men in chains" were commonplace. Ghosts did not like the furniture store that took over the building next. After unseen hands vandalized valuable merchandise with a foul-smelling concoction of urine, feces, and blood a second time, the owner, shotgun in hand, stayed up all night to catch the culprit. Though the vandal failed to appear, the malodorous fluid again covered his inventory. He closed his business.

During the Great Depression the house was a tenement; the families residing here reported seeing a large man in chains and covered with blood walking along the balcony. Children said they were often chased by a woman screaming at them in French. A mother of twins awoke to find a sock shoved into the mouth of one of the infants. Dead, decapitated animals were found in the courtyard. Before long the house was vacant again. In 1969, the mansion was subdivided into twenty apartments, but in 1976 and 1980, its grandeur was restored when architects Koch and Wilson renovated the front portion of the aging building as a private home for Dr. Russell Albright with five apartments at the rear of the building. In 2007, the Lalaurie Mansion was bought by actor Nicolas Cage, who reportedly had his own troubles with disgruntled ghosts; the bank foreclosed on the property in 2009. The mansion is presently for sale.

Ghost hunters and tourists report feeling faint or nauseated near the premises. Some have seen Madame Lalaurie brandishing a whip and chasing a young dark girl across the rear gallery late in the evening. Others report disembodied cries of terror, the splat of objects hitting the pavement, windows being broken, and the raucous sounds of an invisible mob. Photographers have captured ghostly orbs around the roof, but paranormal investigators have not been able to put their modern ghost detection devices to use because of lack of access to the property.

"So," Karolyn said, "you're telling me I just saw a ghost." Ignoring her trepidation, Mae asked, "Do you think the ghost stories about the house will dissuade Ms. Jacob?" Karolyn tried to pull herself together. Maybe she hadn't seen anything at all. It had been a long week. "Well, we'll see if she believes in that series she's working on, won't we? If she thinks ghosts are just Hollywood illusions, she's in for a surprise," Karolyn said. The other agents had said this house would be a difficult sale, but maybe she had found just the right client. "Let's make an appointment for her to see it! What do we have to lose?" Karolyn said. "Well," said Mae, the Million-Dollar Club member, "I like to think about a potential sale in terms of 'what we have to gain!'"

Chapter 8
Soldiers Forever at Griffon House

The old house on Constance Street has been just that, "constant."
Built in the 1800s, the brick-pillared mansion has weathered Civil
War occupation, commercial enterprises, immigration influx,
drugs and gangs, and most recently, Hurricane Katrina. The home
sits near the corner of Euterpe Street, named after the muse of lyri-
cal poetry. The name of the muse, fathered by Zeus, means "giver
of delight," but it can be said that in the early years, there was any-
thing but delight in this homestead. The War Between the States
left a bloody trail through New Orleans history and with it a bas-
tion of ghostly entities that still haunts many places today, includ-
ing Griffon House.

Andy was a history buff working diligently on his next
book about General Benjamin Butler of the Union army. His
attendance at a conference in New Orleans meant he could
gather research from a list of Civil War places he intended to
visit. He couldn't wait to see Griffon House, at least from the
outside. Though it was a private residence now, the house
had been at the center of Union occupation in New Orleans.
He planned to stroll by the old house, taking notes on its
architecture and gardens. He had read the two competing
stories about ghosts appearing in the upstairs window but
didn't put any stock in either version. He didn't believe in
ghosts; he was, after all, a historian. His mission was to get

a firsthand description of the old house to begin chapter three. It was late afternoon before he could get away from the conference, and by the time he finished a light meal, evening hours were approaching. Tomorrow was already booked full of appointments and places to visit. If he didn't get to Constance Street today, he would have to give up seeing the house. Not wanting to do that, he called a taxi from the restaurant and headed toward the Lower Garden District home. He got out at 1447 Constance, and before he could turn around to ask the cab driver to wait the few minutes it would take to complete his mission, the taxi was gone. It was almost dark, but Andy could still see the mansion, envisioning how it must have looked in its heyday. He scribbled a few notes, glad he had come to see the house for himself. As he was looking around for a taxi, he had an eerie feeling that he was being watched. He swung his eyes to the third-story window of Griffon House and saw two figures with blue caps and Union uniforms, staring at him, their lips moving. While his legs went weak, Andy strained to hear what they were saying.

General Benjamin Butler's Union troops swooped in to occupy New Orleans in the early years of the war. By 1862 martial law had been declared and private property commissioned to serve the needs of Union soldiers inhabiting the city. Records indicate that Union troops appropriated the property at 1447 Constance Street, one of the finest houses in the area with fourteen-foot ceilings and spacious rooms, to house men, supplies, even criminals. As soldiers searched the property, they discovered a bloody horror chamber on the third floor. Chained to the walls were about a dozen slaves—dead and near dead. The owner, Adam Griffon, and his family had fled their home just ahead of the approaching Union garrison, leaving their brutally tortured slaves to die. The chained and manacled slaves were suffering from maggot-infested wounds, dehydration, and starvation. The living were removed to a field hospital, and Union soldiers confiscated the house. The ghosts of these wretched slaves haunt Griffon House, as screams and deathly sounds emanate from the walls, echoing up and down the stairway, seeking their revenge on Adam Griffon.

Two equally documented versions of ghostly residents at this address have long been part of New Orleans history. The first story goes that after Federal troops usurped the house, Captain Hugh Devers and Quartermaster Charles Cromley took over the place as their living quarters. They moved their fashionable wives into the house and took advantage of the elegant and lavish lifestyle that New Orleans afforded them. Unfortunately the two men also enjoyed frequenting French Quarter gambling houses. Their downfall came when the men, in over their heads in debt, hatched a plan to rob the Union payroll, which was under their purview. They almost got away with the criminal deed, but General Butler got wind of the purloined payroll. The men knew they had been found out. To escape punishment and disgrace, they decided on a double suicide. They put on their finest Union uniforms and campaign ribbons and spit-polished their boots. After sending their wives off to a fancy ball, the two men climbed the stairs to the third-floor attic where, only a short time before, slaves had been writhing in pain, to carry out their suicide pact. Pointing pistols at each other's chests, the men pulled the triggers simultaneously, two shots ringing out as one. No one ever knew what became of the stolen payroll. Was it hidden in the house or elsewhere? The other side of this tale is that the double suicides were carried out by two Confederate soldiers caught looting while wearing Union uniforms. After their capture and incarceration in the third-floor attic of Griffon House, the Rebels continued to pretend to be Union soldiers, hoping to avoid prosecution by the occupying Union forces. When guards informed them that the order to shoot all looters referred to both Union and Confederate soldiers, they knew they were doomed. Refusing to give Yankee soldiers the pleasure of executing them, the men kept up their charade. They bribed their guards, sympathetic to "Union soldiers" helping themselves to a little Confederate booty, to bring them whiskey and two pistols. The men downed the libation and began to sing. Then they shot each other in the chest, simultaneously. The guards rushed in and found two dead bodies and a river of blood dripping through the floorboards. Manifestations of this drama are part of the ghostly lore that permeates Griffon House history. Neighbors and passersby claim that two soldiers in blue uniforms stand at the third-floor window singing "John Brown's Body" while brandishing a whiskey bottle. Their voices get louder as they reach the chorus: "Glory, glory, hallelujah! His soul's marching on!" Ghostly stories began to circulate almost immediately.

After the Civil War, the house passed through several hands. In the 1920s an old man who rebuilt air conditioners owned it. The man said the house was haunted by strange phenomena. He refused to elaborate on these happenings, and one day the man mysteriously disappeared, never to be seen or heard of again. After that the house became a union hiring hall.

By 1936, the house was a lamp factory. One December night, Calvin, a maintenance worker, stayed late to straighten up the upstairs showroom where employees had been assembling Christmas orders. It was midnight, and the owners were just finishing up downstairs. Suddenly they heard a terrifying scream as Calvin raced down the stairs in panic. He bolted six blocks before he could be stopped for questioning. Calvin told his story in huffs and puffs. "I's cleanin' up, den I heard boots stompin' round da room." Calvin's eyes grew bigger. "But, when I turned ta see who come into da room . . . there was no one, nutin' at all." Calvin took a deep breath and continued, "Then one a dem closet doors swung open and I saw da boots . . . black and shiny-smooth." He gasped for breath, "Dere was no legs in da boots!!" By this time Calvin had worked himself into a frenzy once again. "Den I heard mo' boots, and dey all was comin' right fer me!" Calvin tried to calm down, but then he remembered, "And dey was singin' like dey was drunk, somethin' about 'brown body.' I ran fer da stairs! But, dose voices just followed me." The owners tried to pacify their obviously distraught employee, but nothing, not even an increase in pay, could lure Calvin back to the lamp factory. The house was still a lamp factory in 1946, but neighbors heard and saw crazy things and at night they crossed the street as they hurried by the building. Some reported walking around the block, well out of their way, so as not to pass near the haunted place. A few years after these goings-on, the lamp factory vacated the premises, claiming it was near impossible to keep tenants in the building.

The structure was turned into a boardinghouse for a brief time, but unsettling occurrences brought that chapter to an unseemly end. A widow rented one of the second-floor rooms, and though she found the place quite to her liking, it was not to last. One afternoon as she sat by the window sewing, she noticed a bit of blood on her arm. Thinking it must be an accidental scratch, she wiped the scarlet trickle away. But in an instant, it was back, and then another appeared and another! Trying to find a rational explanation for the bloody spots on her arm, she looked toward the ceiling to see blood oozing through a crack directly above her. As she tried to sort out what was happening, she heard drunken singing coming from the third floor—the faint strains of "John Brown's Body"! She knew the ghost stories and recognized the eerie rendition of the popular Civil War song. She began to yell at the top of her lungs and ran screaming from the house. The woman refused to return. Relatives who came to pack her belongings encountered no dripping blood in the room. But upon leaving with hastily packed trunks, they claimed to see two men in blue uniforms smiling down at them from the attic window. The room was boarded up; no renter could be found to live in the room directly under the attic.

The old house continued to survive the ensuing years. In the 1950s a hurricane leveled the slave quarters in the backyard. When the fallen trees and debris were cleared, a tunnel running under the house to the street was discovered. Civil War–era relics were found: old trunks full of uniforms, slave chains, and other artifacts, but no money or treasure. Neighborhood children often dared one another to enter the house. A group of boys and their two dogs ventured upstairs to the attic, where they saw that the floorboards had been ripped up and the room below was visible. A door suddenly blew open, blasting the intruders with cold air. One of the dogs was uncannily frightened, lost his footing on the exposed floor joist, and fell to his instant death below. The other dog acted so strangely that the boys made a speedy departure, scurrying away even faster when a deep baritone voice behind them belted out, "John Brown's body lies a-mouldering in his grave. . . ."

In the late 1970s, a couple bought the house with the intention of restoring it to its former glory. In an interview, they said they had experienced nothing strange at the old place, but, for some reason or the other, they never occupied the house on Constance Street. Soon after, the neighborhood deteriorated quickly. Many houses in the once-elegant part of town were now dilapidated. Gangs and addicts infiltrated the area and took up residence in many of the decaying structures. Drug lords used the run-down area as a shield for their illegal business. One neighbor related a gripping story about the Griffon House at this time. He said that many of the abandoned houses had become drug havens. But drug kingpins surreptitiously avoided the house at 1447 Constance, claiming to have seen two white men with dark foreboding eyes in "police uniforms" walking through walls and singing "old timey songs"! Even the city's homeless and destitute stayed clear of the residence already claimed by people who may have had been dead for more than a century.

Andy shook off the eerie pall that had enveloped him. Had the heat made him imagine faces in the window? He looked up at the Greek Revival masonry town house, now in the hands of a private owner, and remarked to himself that the area seemed to have turned around. Other Civil

War–era homes in the neighborhood had been renovated; a new bed-and-breakfast down the street announced its opening. Devastation from Hurricane Katrina had given way to hope and progress. Yes, it must have been the heat. No taxi rolled by in the softly fallen darkness, and the sudden drop in temperature alarmed Andy. He looked back at the old house, and his knees went weak again. Two men posted at the upstairs window, muskets thrown over their shoulders, were singing. This time he had no trouble making out the words: "John Brown's body lies a-mouldering in his grave, but his soul keeps marching on."

Chapter 9

The Sultan's Refuge

The imposing Gardette-LePrêtre mansion, infamously known as the Sultan's Palace, is at the heart of one of the city's most mysterious legends. The three-story looming edifice at 716 Dauphine Street on the corner of Orleans Avenue boasts a peculiar amenity in a city that sits below sea level—a half-story raised basement, a rare feature in New Orleans homes. The mansion, unlike most other buildings of its size in the French Quarter, was not designed to house a commercial enterprise on the ground floor and living quarters on the upper floors. It was originally constructed as a single-family residence, a palatial home requiring considerable wealth to furnish and maintain. And so this is where the story of a beloved house and its demise begins and all because of an exotic foreigner who dwelled for just a short time under the delicate hand-carved rosettes that adorned the high ceilings of its opulent rooms.

Mike and Pierre Chase were New Orleans cops. The city's police force had been living under a shroud of negativity since Hurricane Katrina in 2005 when high winds took down electricity lines, water overflowed levees, homes were destroyed, and frightened citizens forgot civility. Police officers were at times kind, helpful, at wit's end, and ruthless. Stories circulated of officers shirking their duties; some were based on truth and some were not. But things were slowly getting back to normal. The French Quarter had escaped much of Mother Nature's wrath, and tourism in the old part of the city was thriving. Mike and Pierre, who had followed in their father's footsteps, loved being police officers in the Crescent City. Most days they were on patrol together; their duties including walking the streets of the Vieux Carré, checking on people and property. They usually started at opposite ends of the area, working inward, and stopping for lunch at midday. When they approached each other, their stomachs were already gurgling, anticipating a bowl of spicy crayfish étouffée or a shrimp po' boy with hot sauce at Felix's. They were just about to turn off Royal onto a side street when suddenly a tourist—they both recognized the "look"—ran up screaming about a sultan and a girl. "Hold on there a minute," Mike began. "Slow down if you want us to understand you." The man dusted off his plaid shirt and straightened his khaki shorts. "Well," he said, "I was just walking over by the old Sultan's Palace, when I looked up and saw a woman being pushed over the balcony by someone in a turban! You need to come right away." Pierre tried to dissuade the man that anything wrong was going on. But the man was insistent: "If you don't come right away, I'm going to the police station to file a report." Mike and Pierre looked at each other; they knew lunch would have to wait. The Sultan was at it again.

In 1836, a Philadelphia dentist, Dr. Joseph Coulon Gardette, moved to New Orleans and contracted with builder Frederick Roy for a grand mansion, the tallest structure in the Vieux Carré at the time. The Greek Revival residence was brick stucco with gutters of copper and included a carriage house. The contract called for wooden beams of the finest quality, high ceilings, and a flagstone courtyard. The door of the first floor was three feet above street level because of the partially underground basement housing a cellar, a bathroom with a marble tub, and an office. Three years later, the handsome property was sold to Jean Baptiste LePrêtre (spelled differently in various records), who proudly displayed the home as a testament to his success. The wealthy Creole banker made the place even more admired by adding luxurious velvet curtains, glittering chandeliers, and cast-iron grillwork to balconies on the second and third floors. The dashing LePrêtre was an influential leader in New Orleans high society. A beautiful aristocratic wife and children enhanced his wealth and power. Music emanated from the top-floor ballroom of the mansion at the center of Creole culture and society. Here, the LePrêtre family resided during the late fall and winter. Planting, growing, and harvesting seasons were spent at their large Mississippi River plantation, rich in rice, corn, tobacco, and slaves.

Near the end of the Civil War, the fortunes of the Creole elite in the South waned. LePrêtre was deeply in debt, and this unfortunate situation led him to consider renting out his French Quarter home. A mysterious Turk who claimed to be a deposed sultan arrived in port and, dressed in royal robes, was received with great respect by the officials of the city. The sultan said that, fearing assassination, he had fled his land, taking with him a full entourage of armed bodyguards, a substantial harem, and his brother's favorite wife. Europe proved to be a fleeting hideaway, and he sailed to America seeking refuge. Turkey's war forays included Italy, Serbia, and Russia, so his story seemed plausible to authorities. The young man needed a large house to accommodate his sizable cadre of men and women. When he offered generous monetary terms for the use of the house, LePrêtre agreed.

LePrêtre cleared out his personal belongings and retreated to his plantation. The sultan used his fortune in gold to transform the Creole town house into an eastern pleasure palace replete with Persian carpets, colorful couches, strewn cushions of rare silks, hand-carved furniture, and beautiful bejeweled chests. Braziers warmed the spacious rooms, incense wafted from the house, exotic music filled the street, and in the courtyard women giggled softly. But no one ever saw the beautiful women. Somber changes were made to the property making it clear visitors were not welcomed: Heavy drapes covered the windows, doors were sealed, and the front gate was permanently chained. Neighbors spoke of menacing behavior and men with curved daggers patrolling the grounds. Tongues began to wag of unbridled orgies, all-night opium parties, and dark, dancing, hedonistic shadows.

One night a terrible storm passed through the city. It was reported later that a strange ship with a crescent banner had slipped into port. In the morning it was gone. Neighbors, confused by the deadly silence at the house, noticed dark trickles of blood oozing under the front door and down the steps. Authorities were called. When they broke down the front door, they were confronted with unspeakable horror: blood-soaked walls and floors, headless bodies, and mutilated limbs. On the grand staircase lay bodies so hacked and scattered they could not be identified. But the sultan's tortured body was found intact. He had been buried alive in the garden, a clutching hand protruding from the freshly covered grave.

No one knows who committed the heinous crimes, but there are three theories. One, nefarious pirates learned of the bountiful treasure and stole into the city during the night to commit the massacres and usurp the valuable gold and jewels. Two, the sultan's crew, fearing being tracked down by the brother back in Turkey, invaded the recluse's home, looted the place, murdered their victims, and dispersed into the murky Louisiana waterways. Third, the sultan's brother avenged the theft of his men, women, and fortune. No one ever claimed the bodies, nor reported any disappearances.

Soon after this horrific episode, the mansion was regarded as haunted, and in 1878 it passed to the Citizens Bank of Louisiana as part of a lawsuit against LePrêtre. Four years later Marie Louise Rousset Oehmichen bought the house from the bank; her husband died that same year. Over the next sixty years the house was bought and sold numerous times. Ultimately the only way an owner could afford the huge house was by dividing it into apartments, and this has been its fate.

For many years the residence was a decaying edifice with its owners making only minor alterations to meet the demands of paying tenants. During the Italian immigration period in the late 1800s, it was used as multi-family dwellings. People credited evil spirits for the unfortunate happenings there. When a woman fell from a top balcony while hanging clothes, her death was blamed on angry ghosts. Tenants, tormented by visions of dismembered men and kept awake by eerie music and terrible screams, claimed to have seen the sultan himself at the foot of their bed in his turban and flowing robes.

The property housed the New Orleans Academy of Art in the late 1940s, and the tales of hauntings continued. Strange sounds were heard at night: music, footsteps on the stairs, and women screaming in pain. Some saw the faces of harem women peering out from upper-floor windows.

When World War II called many of the school's students to service, it became a boardinghouse, then a shelter for vagrants. By the 1950s the building became a reputable apartment complex of nine units, several of which were two-story dwellings, but ghost stories persisted. A respectable tenant with a successful choreography career at the time said in a *Times-Picayune* newspaper interview that she had been startled numerous times by a man in authentic Turkish clothing who would mysteriously appear and disappear in her room. For a while the man seemed harmless enough. Then one night, she heard footsteps running down the hall and blood-curdling screams from the bottom of the staircase. She moved out immediately. In 1966, Jean and Frank D'Amico and Anthony Vesich bought the property, restored it, and refurbished the apartments. The D'Amicos lived in the luxury penthouse suite. When neighbors related the house's bizarre history, the couple passed it off as gossip until one night, while trying to sleep, Jean sensed a presence in the room with her. She looked up and saw a turbaned man standing at the end of her bed; as she reached for the bedside lamp, the figure vanished.

Outwardly, the house on Dauphine Street, with its wrought-iron-laced balconies and cozy courtyard, doesn't reflect the scene of debauchery and carnage that took place there, but inside its elegant walls, slaughtered spirits seem to find little rest. Neighbors hear music late at night in the house; others report the scent of incense coming from the house. Paranormal phenomena related to many restless spirits have been reported in the house: loud, menacing screams, veiled women staring down at the street just after sunset, a man wearing a turban moving quickly across shadowy windows, phantom footsteps, and strangely clad apparitions floating from room to room. Terrible screams pierce the night air as if the carnage were still happening. The house exudes an eerie presence that causes people to cross the street when passing in fear that the sultan may try to add to his cadre.

Mike and Pierre followed the man down Dauphine to the house in question. The luxury apartment complex was still quite an imposing structure. The man pointed up to the balcony where he had seen the girl struggling. Of course, there was nothing and no one to see. But the man insisted he had witnessed a near murder. Pierre asked the man if he had ever been to New Orleans before. "No, never," he said. "Well, why don't we take you to lunch and tell you the story of the Sultan's Palace. Then you can decide if you want to take your story to the station downtown or not." The man was not wavering in his insistence to report the incident, but then the front door opened and a tenant came down the stairs toward them. She greeted the policemen, winking, "Hi, officers. Investigating any more ghostly murders this fine day?" The tourist sighed and, laughingly, decided to take advantage of the free lunch he had been offered. At least he would have some great stories to take back to Omaha.

Chapter 10

Ghostly Guests
of Hotel Monteleone

The celebrated Hotel Monteleone, the "Grande Dame of the French Quarter," doesn't hide the very active spirit world ensconced here. Management takes pride in its resident ghosts as a way to connect to its rich and colorful past. The staff encourages guests to interact with the mostly friendly spirits who have chosen to remain for all eternity on the stately premises. In 2003 the International Society for Paranormal Research was able to identify and contact twelve entities in their earthbound home at the Hotel Monteleone. Generations of guests and staff have told remarkable tales of otherworldly encounters within its nineteenth-century walls. Locals say the French Quarter begins at the Monteleone lobby, which opens onto the pavement at the foot of Royal Street, one of the most elegant and fashionable streets in the Vieux Carré.

Kim and Damien were celebrating Kim's promotion with a weekend in New Orleans. They had reservations at the Hotel Monteleone, as suggested by Mr. Paul, Kim's boss at the architectural firm. The young couple had been awed by the exquisite marble floors and antique furnishings in the lobby and were just as impressed with their room. Kim was an interior designer and had been promoted to the commercial division. Damien had made dinner plans at Antoine's so they quickly unpacked some evening clothes. Kim couldn't wait to take in the city's unique architecture and peer in the windows of antique shops at the beautiful period furnishings that she had only, until now, seen in books and catalogs. Damien was hoping to get to Jackson Square; he had heard it was very romantic.

Kim jumped in the shower while Damien went down to the front desk to get a map of the French Quarter. While her husband was taking his turn in the bathroom, Kim sighed, "Could the weekend be any more perfect?" When she sat on the bed to slide on her new, pointy-toed heels, she noticed something in her shoes. She looked closer . . . it was an earring. *That's odd,* she thought. It definitely wasn't any of the earrings she had packed. In fact, it was a beautiful diamond earring and probably quite expensive. When she noticed a matching earring in the other shoe, she understood completely. She sauntered over to the bathroom door and called out, "Ooh, Dami, they're beautiful." Damien was just getting out of the shower and shot Kim a look. "What's beautiful?" "The earrings, of course," she said. "What a wonderful gift!" "Uh, I hate to tell you this, but I didn't get you any earrings," Damien confessed. The couple was stunned. The only explanation was that a maid or a delivery boy on a mission to surprise a lucky girl had surreptitiously entered and left the earrings in the wrong room, and wrong shoes. "Let's take them to the front desk," Damien said. He felt Kim's disappointment. "I'm sorry I didn't think to get you a gift," he said. "That's okay," Kim said. "Let's go to dinner." It was supposed to be the best weekend ever; now Damien wasn't so sure.

Antonio Monteleone, a proud Sicilian of noble lineage, operated a prosperous shoe factory in Italy. But the young man wanted more excitement and adventure than the family business could offer. Lured by the American dream, Monteleone left his beloved homeland behind and arrived in New Orleans in 1880. Here he opened a small cobbler's shop on Royal Street, where many commercial enterprises were flourishing. The entrepreneur enjoyed success from the outset and in 1886 expanded his business holdings by purchasing the nearby sixty-four-room Commercial Hotel on the corner of Royal and Iberville Streets. This was the beginning of the Monteleone dynasty. In 1903, business was booming and an adjacent building was purchased, expanding the hotel by thirty rooms. Five years later, more buildings were bought and Antonio expanded again, this time adding three hundred rooms. He commissioned Albert Toledano and Victor Wogan, two of the few architects in New Orleans using an ornate commercial style. Then he changed the name of the hotel to the Monteleone.

Antonio died in 1913, having lived long enough to see his hotel become one of the premier establishments in the city. Son Frank took on managing the hotel and oversaw the addition of two hundred more rooms. By 1926, the Hotel Monteleone could boast that all its rooms had ceiling fans and radios! During the Great Depression, which began in 1929, the Monteleone family held on tightly to their grand hotel, the only one in the city to stay open during the stock market crash. In 1930, the Monteleone was the first hotel in New Orleans to treat guests to air conditioning in its luxuriant lobby. By 1954, though, the old buildings were showing their age. The original, decaying structures were torn down, and a new Hotel Monteleone, emulating its original

Beaux Arts grand style, rose from the rubble. New dining and entertaining spaces sporting glittering chandeliers, polished marble floors, and gilded fixtures made the hotel even more popular. Celebrities Liberace and Nelson Eddy entertained locals and guests in the new Swan Room. Frank died in 1958, and son William took over, adding more floors to the hotel as well as the Sky Terrace with swimming pool and cocktail lounges. A fourth generation of Monteleones runs the hotel today, with a fifth generation waiting in the wings.

Well-known celebrities such as Paul Newman and Joanne Woodward stayed at the hotel to enjoy its original "Vieux Carré" cocktail in the piano lounge. More recent celebrity guests include Michael Jordan, Dennis Quaid, Greg Allman, and Sally Struthers. The Carousel Piano Bar & Lounge resembles a real-life carousel with bright lights, opulent filigree, and circus motifs. The bar and twenty-five seats around it make a complete revolution every fifteen minutes, turning on two thousand steel rollers pulled by a one-quarter horsepower motor. During the 1950s and 1960s, the bar also housed the Swan Room, a nightclub hosting popular musicians like Louis Prima, Etta James, and Pete Fountain. The Monteleone is also known for the literary giants who found a home away from home in its flamboyantly decorated rooms. Tennessee Williams wrote *The Rose Tattoo* while at the hotel, and his grandfather, the Reverend Walter Dakin, stayed here in 1958. Ernest Hemingway mentions the Monteleone in his short story, "Night before Battle." William Faulkner spent his honeymoon here in 1929 and also stayed when he was writing his novel *The Sound and the Fury*. Faulkner's biographer reports that the Monteleone was the author's "favorite hotel on earth." Truman Capote loved staying at the hotel and was known to do his share of writing while sitting in the Carousel Bar listening to live New Orleans jazz. On *The Tonight Show* Capote claimed he was born in the Monteleone. His pregnant mother was staying at the hotel, but she safely made it to the hospital for Truman's birth. To reciprocate the love shown by these famous authors, the hotel has named suites in their honor: the William Faulkner Suite, the Truman Capote Suite, the Tennessee Williams Suite, and the Ernest Hemingway Penthouse Suite. Sherwood Anderson and his wife, Elizabeth, lived here in 1921. Winston Groom, author of *Forrest Gump,* also stayed here. The Monteleone is referenced in Rebecca Wells's *Divine Secrets of the Ya-Ya Sisterhood,* Stephen Ambrose's *Band of Brothers,* and Eudora Welty's *A Curtain of Green.* Anne Rice and John Grisham have also stayed at the hotel. In 1999, the Hotel Monteleone joined an exclusive list of hotels in the country to receive the prestigious Literary Landmark designation.

Ghosts of former employees roam freely through the Monteleone, and apparently they liked working for the hotel so much in their real life, they continue their services after death. A ghostly male entity tinkers day and night with the hand-carved mahogany clock that stands center stage in the grand lobby. He is thought to be one of the artisans who built the clock. A young boy who probably worked as a bell-hop for the hotel likes to play tag in the hallways with the specter of a young girl. There are "doormen" at the hotel's restaurant, Le Café, that open and close the locked doors, always around 7 p.m. One spirit is a maintenance man who wants the door closed; the other is a waiter, who prefers the door open. "Ms. Clean" came from a long line of housekeepers; her mother, grandmother, and great-grandmother were all maids at the Monteleone. She has been spotted in guest rooms, cleaning up after present-day maids who don't live up to her expectations for cleanliness. A man encountered regularly is Red, often seen puttering around the place and trying to keep everything in working order. He identifies himself as the hotel engineer as he makes his daily rounds. Red reportedly died in the hotel. The Monteleone has honored this dedicated employee with a cocktail named after him, called Red's Rum.

Past guests also hang around. William Wildemere is still on an after-life vacation, though he died on holiday in the hotel. During Mardi Gras a nude man wearing only a feathered mask surprises guests as he searches in vain for his own room. A jazz singer belts out energetic New Orleans tunes, entertaining startled couples in their rooms in the middle of the night. A dour-looking businessman named John, supposedly from Tennessee, who visited in the 1920s, also makes an occasional appearance as does a woman called Helen who thinks she is still alive despite having no head. Star-crossed lovers are said to roam the premises.

The Monteleone has no thirteenth floor. After the twelfth floor comes the fourteenth floor, which, paranormal investigators say, must have been popular with families over the years as many entities of children are seen running and playing in these hallways where temperatures can instantly drop to bone-chilling iciness. Unseen hands press elevator buttons, and when the doors open, no one is waiting. Curious guests who get off are led down a hallway that grows colder and colder, nearing ghostly children at play. Other guests complain of sleepless nights due to noises from a children's birthday party; in the morning they are assured there was no party. Another little lost girl roams the hotel, pleading for help before vanishing into thin air.

In the late 1890s Josephine and Jacques Begere stayed in the hotel. They brought their three-year-old son, Maurice, and his nanny with them. On the way back from the Grand French Opera House on Bourbon Street, disaster struck. The horse pulling the buggy in which the couple was riding was suddenly spooked, throwing a startled Jacques out of the carriage to his death. Some say their young son caught yellow fever in the city and died at the hotel. Josephine, distraught over losing her husband and then her son, never recovered and died a year later. A hopeful Maurice wanders the fourteenth floor, where the family had been staying, searching for his parents. He often stands at the foot of guests' beds dressed in a striped shirt. He doesn't mind his picture being taken, but photos display only a black formless shape where the young boy had stood. These frequent phantom guests are remembered in namesake hotel drinks: Maurice's Madness, Solemn John, and Headless Helen.

The Travel Channel's *Weird Travels* featured the otherworldly activities discovered by International Society for Paranormal Research investigators at the Hotel Monteleone on its episode, "Spirits of the South." Films, such as *Double Jeopardy,* and several television programs have been filmed here. A wax statue of Antonio Monteleone was unveiled for the hotel's 125th anniversary.

The man at the front desk, "Eddie" by his badge, did not seem shocked when Kim and Damien showed him the diamond earrings. In fact, he bounced them in his hand a few times, said a polite "Thank you," and stashed them under the counter. Kim was not sure he understood how valuable the earrings were. "You know those are real diamonds?" she said, continuing, "And do you know who put them in my shoes?" Eddie straightened his tie and smoothed his hair. "Yes, ma'am, I do." "Well?" Kim asked. "It's like this," the young man explained. "We have a ghost here in the hotel who thinks it's funny to take these earrings and put them in guests' shoes. It happens over and over. We'll put the earrings in the hotel safe, but the ghost will somehow get them again and trick another guest."

Kim and Damien walked out into the early evening air to clear their heads. Kim tried to be upbeat, but she had really loved those earrings. The couple strolled down Royal Street, Kim peering through the wide windows at the lovely antiques. Damien suddenly had an idea. He grabbed Kim's hand and pulled her into the shop across the street. "What are you doing?" asked Kim, looking around at the beautiful jewelry. "It may not have been my idea," Damien said, "but I'm getting you a pair of gorgeous earrings to celebrate your promotion." Kim saw just the ones she wanted and pointed to them. She thanked her husband profusely for the awesome gift but made a mental note to herself to also thank the "ghost of earrings" when she got back to the hotel.

Chapter 11

Have a Cigar at the Columns Hotel

The Columns Hotel at 3811 St. Charles Avenue allows visitors and locals to step back to an era when chivalry was an art and women floated along the Garden District in flounced antebellum dresses. The hotel offers a "southern" patio where friends can sip mint juleps and Ramos gin fizzes in warm evening breezes. Inside, the dark, mahogany bar beckons weary sightseers to rest a while. The hotel is decorated with elegant antique furniture, velvet couches, and Persian tapestries. A beautiful old staircase leading to the rooms above seems to reach toward a world beyond the present. The spacious interior is graced by cozy sitting rooms on both sides of the entry where guests can rest and converse about the happenings of the day. New Orleanians love this impressive Colonial mansion with its inviting grand front gallery; many of them have celebrated wedding vows here while iconic streetcars rattle up and down the avenue. This hotel is so beautiful that some of its nineteenth-century former owners have just plain refused to move out.

Laurence lounged on the wide front veranda of the Columns Hotel, legs sprawled under the table, jacket open and tie loose. It had been a great day, an important contract had been signed, and he was ready to relax. In just a few minutes, his wife, Beth, would arrive, and he had a special dinner planned for their anniversary. He ordered another drink and then, softly and slowly, drifted off to the distant past. He supposed it was the old hotel that carried him back in time. He was tired; it had been a long week. He closed his eyes and imagined what it was like to have lived in days gone by. Hesitating to wake from this soothing dreamlike state, he smiled when the well-dressed man asked if he needed anything. "Just my wife," Laurence teased. "Can you make her appear?" "Not really, sir," said the dapper man, grinning broadly, as he held out his hand, offering a La Belle Creole, "but how about enjoying some local tobacco while you wait?" "Thanks," said Laurence, putting the cigar to his lips, not even questioning why it was already lit. He took a few puffs and relaxed even more, if that was possible. "Darling," a soft voice said, "are you asleep?" It was his wife. "Where's my cigar?" he inquired, startled. "I knew I smelled cigar smoke when I came up. You know I hate that smell," Beth was annoyed. Laurence looked around, but there was no cigar in sight, no ashtray, no sign at all, except the wink from the man near the front door, who had handed him the cigar just a few minutes ago. Then, poof, the man vanished into thin air. Laurence was taken aback for a second, but he had an explanation. . . . *Maybe I'm still dreaming,* he thought. Beth, in the meantime, had started fussing about the kids and getting out of the house on time and he knew he was not dreaming anymore. So who was the smiling man?

Simon, the eldest son of Joseph Hernsheim and Ricka Katzenstein, born in 1839, made his mark early on the New

Orleans commercial scene. By the time he was twenty, the young man was owner of a lucrative enterprise. S. Hernsheim & Bros. Co., run by the Hernsheim brothers, Simon, Isidore, and Joseph, and businessman Sigmund Belmont, was supplying tobacco to major markets in Europe. When the Civil War called, he enlisted in the Confederate army. After the war, Reconstruction was tough for New Orleans; Federal occupation took its toll. But by the 1880s things were improving. New Orleans was fast becoming the primary tobacco center in the country. Tobacco factories were springing up, mostly in the French Quarter, and Hernsheim's enterprise led the way in sales, employee benefits, and working conditions. In 1882, five years after the last Yankee troop left the city, Hernsheim built the five-story La Belle Creole Cigar & Tobacco Factory on the corner of Magazine and Julia Streets, where more than a thousand men and women worked to turn out twenty-five million tobacco products. It was the largest factory in the city at the time. Business was so good that the next year Simon contracted to build his dream home on exclusive St. Charles Avenue. His dreams were large scale. Plans for the mansion were drawn up by Thomas Sully, a New Orleans native who had studied and trained in New York and Texas. Sully would become known as the king of architecture in the area, designing more homes on St. Charles Avenue than any other individual. Hernsheim's Italianate chateau was known for its distinctive tower rising about the roof and its beautiful arch-covered walkways. Hernsheim and his wife, Ida, moved into the residence upon completion in 1883, looking forward to many years of entertaining friends and guests in the comfortable receiving rooms and spacious ballroom.

By 1892, the factory was putting out more than forty million cigars made of Cuban tobacco and perique pipe tobacco from leaves grown solely in St. James Parish, in southeastern Louisiana. But the good times were not to last. In 1895 Simon lost both his dear wife and his sister, Henrietta. It seems he could not get over the devastating losses, and early in 1898, his death was reported in the *New York Times*, citing suicide by ingesting cyanide of potassium, one of the most dangerous cyanides. His death was attributed to his profound grief over the loss of family members and other personal problems. The Hernsheim empire faded soon after Simon's death, and it was not long before New Orleans itself waned as a cigar capital due to increased labor costs, import taxes, and problems with suppliers.

Beginning in 1898, Hernsheim's dream mansion passed to a series of owners, who also used it as a family home. The structure suffered greatly in the 1915 hurricane, losing its tower forever. It underwent significant renovation; columns were added at this time, giving the building its current characteristic motif and namesake.

The Feld family bought the home in 1917 and turned it into an upscale boardinghouse that sheltered elite New Orleanians for many years. In 1953 the old mansion was sold again, and this time it became a hotel. In 1978, the controversial film *Pretty Baby*, with Brooke Shields, was filmed here, and the Columns Hotel was transformed into an early twentieth-century bordello. In 1980, Jacques and Claire Creppel bought the hotel, restored it to its original grand style, and continue to run it today. It remains the only one of Sully's houses in the Italianate style still standing.

Many friendly and extremely well-mannered ghosts enjoy their stay at the Columns Hotel, perhaps reinvigorated over the years by the restoration and renovations, which are said to stir up energies and entities left behind in old homes. It seems Hernsheim has remained on the premises of his three-story mansion and still enjoys the home he built from the spoils of the golden age of American cigars. He acts as a gracious host in his home of antique armoires, lovely fireplaces, and period bathtubs. Guests have described a well-dressed gentleman who personally visits the individually "themed" rooms, checking on guests and inquiring if they need anything special to make their stay more memorable. When they assure him everything is more than satisfactory, the apparition disappears into thin air.

Many guests have reported the presence of a lovely woman who floats through the ballroom and roams the gardens, describing her as a "Woman in White." This figure clothed only in white likes to walk around but keeps to herself; she doesn't want to bother anyone. A little girl— no one can pinpoint exactly who she is or why she has remained at the residence—wanders on the third floor near the balcony. She appears to be injured in some way, either by disease or accident.

Spirits enjoy their days and nights surrounded by the past. Albertine's Tea Room has beautiful overhead fans and concave mirrors with a touch of Victorian fanciness, including French-stained glass. The Victorian Lounge, originally the family dining room, resembles a traditional pub with dark woodwork and luxurious bronze chandeliers. Celebrities Cameron Diaz, John Goodman, Michael Jordan, Clint Eastwood, Rod Stewart, Brooke Shields, and Harry Connick Jr. have all enjoyed a drink at the beautiful bar. A sunburst stained-glass skylight floods the impressive mahogany stairway, which is graced by mural walls. This European-style guesthouse with its Old World elegance overlooks the St. Charles trolley line and is on the National Register of Historic Places.

Laurence quieted his wife's fussing. "I have a surprise for you," he said. He took Beth's hand and escorted her to the patio. "I've arranged with the babysitter to stay overnight with the kids," he said. "We'll stay here, at the Columns—sort of a getaway evening for us." Beth was delighted. They sat on the patio and ordered the Sazerac Cocktail, whose pre–Civil War recipe had earned it the title of official drink of New Orleans. When the dashing man Laurence had met earlier sidled over to their table, Laurence recognized him immediately. "Looks like you found your wife, sir," he said. "Yes, indeed I did," Laurence said. The man carefully and silently slipped a cigar under a napkin, saying, "Perhaps for later, monsieur." Then he strolled off as surreptitiously as he had arrived. Beth seemed uncharacteristically distracted. Laurence started to explain, "That man . . ." "What man?" said Beth, trying to concentrate on the small talk. Laurence was dumbstruck. "Didn't you see that impeccably dressed man talking to me just now?" he stammered. "Oh, dear, I guess not," she replied. "I was too busy watching that woman dressed all in white walking around in circles in the garden. See her? Over there. She's strolling round and round. . . ."

Part Two

HAUNTED RESTAURANTS, EATERIES, AND BARS

Native New Orleanians, residents, and visitors to the "City That Care Forgot" have something in common. They appreciate excellent food, great company, and, of course, potent spirits. The city is replete with fine restaurants, from the casual to the most elegant, serving local delicacies with panache and flair. Antoine's and Arnaud's in the French Quarter are world-famous dining establishments that still use decades-old secret recipes for their delectable French dishes. Commander's Palace in the Garden District caters to an "American" palate offering traditional favorites and unique Southern charm.

And now to the spirits. Saunter up to the bar at Pat O'Brien's, Lafitte's Blacksmith Shop, or the Old Absinthe House, and name your poison. Whether imbibing expensive wine, a cool mint julep, a rum hurricane, or a simple sweet ice tea, you will feel your cares lessen a little, rose-colored glasses painting the harsh world in a softer hue. O'Flaherty's is closed, but like all old places in New Orleans, the property will reinvent a new future for itself. There's lots of great company to be had in all these places. Strangers become friends, servers transform into travel experts, and bartenders double as personal confidants. There's no need to be alone in New Orleans. Just smile, order a round of drinks, and "laissez les bons temps rouler!"

Chapter 12

The Well-Dressed Patriarch at Antoine's

Antoine's, the oldest family-owned and -operated restaurant in the United States, is the pride of the Alciatore family tree and the epitome of fine dining in New Orleans. Easily the most recognizable French Quarter restaurant in the world, this exquisite throwback to the glory days of elegant dining attracts tourists from around the globe but also boasts a large and loyal local clientele. The progenitor of the restaurant—the home of Oysters Rockefeller, Pompano en Papillote, and Eggs Sardou—is credited with creating the American equivalent of hors d'oeuvres, now referred to as "appetizers." After a fourteen-million-dollar renovation following wind and rain damage sustained in Hurricane Katrina in 2005, Antoine's is once again considered the most precious jewel in the crown of New Orleans eateries.

Danette and Jan decided to surprise their sister, Debbie, with a fantastic birthday celebration at none other than Antoine's in the French Quarter. After all, she was turning fifty, and that certainly deserved a delicious meal and a bottle of fine wine. The women met outside the restaurant at 713 St. Louis Street. Danette had come prepared to share some history of the restaurant and, through a friend of hers who knew one of the waiters, had managed to schedule a private tour of the history-laden establishment. As Jan gave their name to the hostess, Marshall appeared and gallantly whisked them off through the main dining room and up the stairs. "Let's start our little tour up here," he began. The women learned all about the Rex Room dedicated to the King of Mardi Gras and peeked in at the memorabilia, including bejeweled crowns and scepters from past royalty. Next they visited the 1840 Room styled as a period private dining area aglow in a warm red motif. Marshall then headed them toward the Mystery Room. Jan, intrigued by the historical memorabilia, felt eerily connected to an earlier age. She glanced over her shoulder and smiled at the obviously refined man sporting a well-cut retro tuxedo as he turned the brass doorknob and entered the room to her right. Danette had done her research and asked Marshall, "Where is the Japanese Room?" "Well," he said, "it's just over there, but it's not set up for visitors. Sorry." Jan followed his gesture and raised her eyebrows. "Well, I just saw someone go in there," she volunteered. "Oh, no, I'm afraid not," Marshall said. "It's been locked up for weeks," he added, pointing to the secured bolt on the door. Danette and Debbie looked at their sister's face, suddenly gone ashen, and knew immediately something was amiss. . . .

By the 1830s New Orleans was a bustling cosmopolitan city, cotton was "king," and the Mississippi River was a portal to the world, but because there were few fine restaurants, most Creoles dined at home. However, that was soon to change. In 1838, French immigrant Antoine Alciatore left his homeland and arrived in New York to open a restaurant. Faced with insurmountable obstacles in the overpopulated city, he began to look for a new place to fulfill his life's ambition.

The Paris of the New World, New Orleans, caught his attention, and by 1840 the twenty-seven-year-old restaurateur had become part of the city's culinary landscape. He worked first for the St. Charles Hotel, one of the finest luxury hotels in the city, where a young Louis Moreau Gottschalk, soon to be a renowned American composer and virtuoso pianist, gave his informal public debut. Antoine was at home in the French-speaking city of aristocrats and soon opened his own boardinghouse, Pension Alciatore, and restaurant. When this enterprise promised success, he sent for his fiancée and her sister, still in New York, to join him in the Crescent City. The couple was married, and the family set about the business of building a restaurant legacy. The budding restaurant appealed to the city gentry, and as it outgrew its small quarters, Antoine looked to expand. He went about acquiring the Miltenberger place and some neighboring property just a block away, down St. Louis Street, between Bourbon and Royal Streets. He knocked out some walls and added a cast-iron gallery and mansard roof in 1870 to create the establishment known as Antoine's today. From the beginning Antoine was committed to offering high-quality food and drink and providing an exquisite dining experience to his customers. In a well-tailored tuxedo, he greeted and welcomed the wealthiest and most prominent citizens in and around New Orleans to his culinary artistry.

But his success did not forestall bad news. The restaurateur was in bad health, and wanting to return to his homeland to die, Antoine left for France in 1874, leaving the management of the restaurant in his wife's hands. He died shortly after arriving in France, but it seems his spirit, not to be held captive abroad, traveled the high seas and found its way back to the French Quarter.

Antoine's son, Jules, was schooled in the culinary arts by his mother, who wanted him to continue in his father's footsteps. After six years of apprenticeship, she sent Jules to France, where the young man worked in the finest kitchens of Paris, Strasbourg, and Marseilles. Jules returned to New Orleans in 1887 as chef at the famous Pickwick Club, a highly regarded gentlemen's organization at the corner of Canal and Carondelet Streets. It was named for the celebrated club in Charles Dickens's *The Pickwick Papers,* a popular collection of humorous adventure tales. Several Pickwickians had been Louisiana state convention members who voted for secession from the Union on January 26, 1861. It was the only New Orleans social club to stay open during the Civil War and is still active today.

Jules was summoned by his mother, who felt the young man was ready to lead Antoine's into the next century. And he did, indeed. Jules was a genius in the kitchen, creating the dish Oysters Rockefeller, so named because of the richness of the sauce. The original recipe remains a closely guarded Antoine's secret. Jules married Althea Roy, daughter of George Roy, founding father and prominent planter in Royville, later renamed Youngsville. Their daughter, Marie Louise, would be known in the twentieth century as Antoine's "grande dame" and their son, Roy Louis, would eventually take over the family business in 1934. Roy Louis Alciatore managed Antoine's through World War II and is responsible for the closing of the legendary Japanese Room. In the early 1900s, Japanese decor was a trendy style. Homes and businesses were decorated with Japanese motifs, paintings, porcelain, gewgaws, and the like. The Japanese Room upstairs was popular with trendsetters who felt a table here set them apart from the common diners down in the main room. Then came December 7, 1941, and the bombing of Pearl Harbor by the Japanese. Roy Louis stormed up to the Japanese Room, bolted the door, and gave orders for it to remain locked indefinitely. Some say the room had not even been properly cleaned of table crumbs or its chairs straightened, but no matter, no one was to go in, ever. The restaurant could have filled the room with paying guests, but it remained bolted. Roy Louis also opened the 1840 Room, decorated as a fashionable private dining room of the period; it still contains impressive antiques such as the great silver duck press and a Parisian cookbook from 1659.

In 1972, after nearly forty years of opening and closing the restaurant each day, Roy Louis died. Meanwhile Marie Louise had married William Guste and their sons, William Jr. (who served as attorney general of Louisiana) and Roy Sr. became the fourth Alciatore generation to serve the city's elite from the kitchen of a now very famous Antoine's restaurant. In 1975 Roy Sr.'s son, Roy Jr., became the proprietor and ran Antoine's until 1984. By this time, ill-feeling toward the Japanese had eased, the man who had brazenly shut off the room was no longer alive to exercise his iron restraint, and the door to the Japanese Room was finally opened. The decor was stunning, but much restoration was needed. Artists around the city were commissioned to painstakingly restore the room to its former glory, delicately hand-painting the decaying ceiling and wallpaper. William Guste Jr.'s son, Bernard, fifth generation, is in control today along with Roy Louis's daughter Yvonne Alciatore Blount.

Antoine's excellent French-Creole cuisine attracted famous guests, like Franklin Roosevelt, Herbert Hoover, General George S. Patton, Judy Garland, Bob Hope, Al Jolson, and Pope John Paul II, whose pictures line the walls. Most celebrities like Tom Cruise, Elizabeth Taylor, Julia Roberts, Ben Hogan, and Bill Gates enter the private dining areas through a hidden hallway that runs alongside the restaurant. Antoine's antique leaded glass windows, sheer curtains, and well-worn tile floors run through several buildings divided into fifteen dining rooms, some of which are small, intimate spaces tucked away in corners both upstairs and downstairs. The Hermes Room has hosted dinners for five US presidents.

Many say that Antoine Alciatore still guides the decisions made behind the closed door of Antoine's inner sanctum. His presence is palpably felt by the new generation of family members who confirmed sightings and believe their ancestor is watching over the establishment as they lead Antoine's into yet another century and a different era. Changes have come to Antoine's. The menu has been pared down, and English translations of the French Creole cuisine have been added. The Hermes Bar has opened, the first bar in the restaurant's history, and a new Jazz Brunch has been added. In an interview, Yvonne Alciatore Blount said, "We very much feel a weight of responsibility" for the changes being made. One story goes that a restaurant manager was making some dinner preparations in the hallway upstairs and noticed a busboy enter the Japanese Room. He thought this behavior odd and attempted to follow the young man into the room, but when he turned the handle, he found the door was locked. He immediately went for the key, unlocked the door, and found the room empty. Another time he was taking some important papers upstairs to the office. As he started to climb the stairs, he noticed a glowing figure on the top landing. Then puff, the apparition was gone.

Guests and employees often describe incidents when the original owner, Antoine, appears dressed in a tuxedo to apparently keep watch over the daily activities. A staff member claims to have seen a figure entering, very businesslike, the Mystery Room. This room was popular during Prohibition because it was only accessible through a hidden door in the ladies' restroom. Here gin was poured illegally and lavishly into coffee cups for local imbibers. Thinking at first it was the headwaiter on an errand, he followed the man into the room to ask a question. But when he got there, no one was about. Later, as he recounted his story to some of the other waiters, he was asked to describe the man he had seen. The seasoned waiters realized the young man had described Antoine Alciatore. The Mystery Room has its share of ghostly activity; apparently many want to return to the place where alcohol became a secret seductress. Another story involves a cashier who reported seeing a transparent specter of Antoine, in his tuxedo, looking over the till, as if he was satisfied with the day's counting.

An old structure such as Antoine's is full of good memories, and ghosts are bound to hang around. Apparitions of elegantly dressed men and women in nineteenth-century clothing appear frequently in the mirrors of the men's room and ladies' room. A specter of a young woman in period dress has been spotted in the "wine alley," a 165-foot stone corridor lined with wine racks and fed by precise air-conditioning systems. Cold spots, the kind associated with other-world personalities, have been encountered in almost every part of the restaurant. The ghosts at Antoine's are friendly; many seemingly just want to stay connected to a place where they enjoyed good times and good food.

Jan demanded to know more about the man she had seen enter the room Marshall had called the Japanese Room. She knew what she had seen. "I know I saw a man go in there," she stammered, pointing to the door on her right. Marshall drew a deep breath and began to relate his own experiences of a ghostly Antoine figure often seen checking up on his restaurant and staff. As he described the dapper man, dressed in elegant evening wear, Jan nodded her head. She was not sure she believed the tall ghost tales Marshall was sharing, but then he added an intriguing side note. "It's been documented," he said, "that when Antoine, sickly and frail, departed for France to die, he whispered to his wife that though his death was imminent, he hoped to see her again someday." The silence was absolute. Marshall continued, "Perhaps he hoped he could come back from the spirit world to watch over his precious restaurant." Jan paused and thought, yes, and that's exactly what had happened.

Chapter 13

Ghostly Neighbors
on St. Peter Street

Three very old buildings stand next to each other; they have been neighbors for a long time. All have played a major role in the tumultuous history of New Orleans. It's often difficult to trace specific addresses and owners of the oldest of properties as official documents are a mixture of French, Creole, Spanish, and English. Names have been spelled differently in translation, Spanish clerks attempted to interpret French names, Creole clerks struggled with putting Spanish pronunciations in writing, and foreign-sounding names were sometimes made to sound less harsh to French ears. Records are often hard to decipher. With that in mind, it's easy to understand how three buildings in one block of St. Peter Street have been confused over time. This trio of historic structures dates back to the 1700s when New Orleans was a French city trying desperately to live up to the cultural and social expectations of its inhabitants. Their stories, despite contradictory documentation, are important.

"Girls Weekend" was set, two days and two nights in the French Quarter. Marcia and Jill would drive over from Mandeville, and Dana and Jamie would come together from Baton Rouge. No one could leave until after work on Friday, so it would be dinnertime when they arrived in the city. They decided to meet at Pat O's on St. Peter Street and have dinner at the Courtyard Restaurant. Dana and Jamie arrived just after 6 p.m. and ordered a Hurricane to start the weekend off right while they were waiting for their friends. By 6:30 p.m. they were getting worried, and no one was answering her phone. "I'm going to the ladies' room," Dana said. "We'll decide what to do when I get back." Jamie waved the waiter over; she might as well order another drink. At first the waiter didn't respond, and when he finally came over to the table, he was definitely distraught. "What's the matter, er . . . Lynden?" Jamie asked, taking his name from the badge on his shirt. "I can't find my green jacket, and we are supposed to wear it while we are serving," Lynden said. "This is my first night, and I don't want to get in trouble already." Jamie felt sorry for the young man and politely scanned the courtyard for a wayward green jacket. Unbelievably, she spotted something near the fountain and pointed. "Could that be it?" she asked. The novice waiter walked over to the wadded bundle and straightened it out against his chest. He checked inside the jacket and walked back to Jamie, showing her his name in black marker. Jamie laughed and ordered her drink. Dana was back, and before Jamie could tell her about Lynden and the green jacket, her friend started a story of her own. It seems she had been startled by someone laughing in one of the stalls, but when she peeked under the door, there were no feet. She pushed the door open, and the cubicle was empty. She had fled back down the stairs. They already had some stories to tell Marcia and Jill, who were now walking up to the table. "You'll probably think I've had too much to drink," Dana said, but she began her story anyway. "No, wait," Marcia said. "Do you know why we were late?" The girls looked blankly in response. "Let me tell you what Jill and I saw over at Preservation Hall as we passed by," Marcia said.

The building at 718 St. Peter Street was first owned by François Collell. He sold the property in 1792 to a prominent planter, Etienne-Marie de Flechier, who built a plaster-facade town house for his family. In 1817 the widow Flechier (formerly Françoise Dussan de la Croix) sold the property to John Garnier, a brickmaker of some repute. Many years later and down the street from this property, B. H. "Pat" O'Brien was operating a Prohibition speakeasy called Mr. O'Brien's Club Tipperary. Its doors were only opened to an exclusive few patrons who knew the password, "Storm's Brewin'." After the repeal of Prohibition in 1933, O'Brien moved his now legal club across the street to the 600 block of St. Peter. But soon the popular bar needed more room. In 1942, O'Brien and his friend Charlie Cantrell bought the 1792 building at 718 St. Peter with its old carriageway entrance and aged slate flooring. Crossed muskets representing every country that once flew its flag over the city decorate the now world famous Pat O'Brien's. Pat O's, as it is called by locals, is famous for its signature drink, the "Hurricane," a potent, fruity concoction of rum and passion fruit syrup, garnished with an orange slice and served in a tall glass shaped like a hurricane lamp. It was created during World War II when bar owners were required to purchase large quantities of rum in order to get scarce distilled spirits. Whiskey, bourbon, and scotch were in short supply because grains and sugars went to troops abroad. Rum from the Caribbean islands was plentiful.

Pat O's specialty drinks include the Cyclone, the Tropical Depression, and the alcohol-free Eye of the Hurricane. Under the management of George Oechsner Jr. and his son, Sonny, Pat O's has become the most popular bar in the city. Patrons dance in the aisles to dueling copper-covered twin baby grand pianos in the Piano Lounge. The flaming water fountain in the courtyard dazzles other guests, who are served by waitresses and waiters in Pat O's signature colors, white and green. Pat O's claims to sell more alcohol per square foot than any other establishment in the country. Today the building that houses the Pat O'Brien's complex at 718 St. Peter is called the Casa de Flechier/Pat O'Brien's property.

Just next door at 726 St. Peter is an equally well-known establishment. Don Antonio Faisendieu purchased this property from Don Geronimo Gros around 1750 and changed the private residence into a tavern called Faisendieu's Posada. In the ensuing years it has served as an inn, a photo studio, and an art gallery. Since 1961 it has been known as Preservation Hall, a showplace of New Orleans music. Clouded portraits of early musicians hang on the old walls, and an ornate iron gate protects its tropical courtyard. Founded by Allan and Sandra Jaffe, the hall honors New Orleans jazz. At night, the hall fills to capacity. Allan Jaffe died in 1987, and his son Benjamin, a graduate of Oberlin Conservatory, took over as musical director. He plays bass and tuba with the band and works on its small record label and website. A permanent funeral wreath in the carriageway marked the passing of Narvin Kimball, a banjoist and the last founding member of the band, who died at age ninety-seven in 2006. Erle Stanley Gardner, author of the *Perry Mason* novels, lived in an apartment above the hall. *The Case of the Singing Skirt* was dedicated to Dr. Nicholas M. Chetta, the New Orleans coroner. An early document says the property was "united with the property of Marie de Flechier" on one side and with "le spectacle" on the other. Another official document says the property lies between that of "Don Esteban Flechier" and "El Coliseo, the Playhouse." Confusing? The building at 726 St. Peter is cited today as the Faisendieu's Posada/Preservation Hall property.

The property at 732 St. Peter was first owned by Juan Doreto del Postigo, who sold it at public auction in 1790 to Louis Chevalier de Macarty. A year later, Don Luis Alessandro bought the property from Macarty plus an adjoining piece from Geronimo Gros. The address became that of El Coliseo, a playhouse where a troupe of actors, driven from the Saint-Domingue slave rebellion, gave performances under the direction of Louis Blaize Tabary, an educated French colonist. In 1796, horse-drawn carriages brought patrons to the city's first opera on record, André Ernest Grétry's *Sylvain*. Bernardo Coquer continued as manager until the playhouse closed. When the playhouse opened again, it was called La Salle de Comédie and was shut down off and on, due to bawdy outbreaks, insulting songs aimed at authorities, and management and personnel crises. After the 1803 Louisiana Purchase, the name was changed again, this time to La Théâtre de la Rue St. Pierre, but though the name had been changed, the rowdiness had not and it, too, was closed down. In 1806 the theater went by the name Le Spectacle de la Rue Saint Pierre and featured regular performances of French dramatic works, ballets, classical drama, and pantomimes. A year later, a riot broke out in the theater, and it was again closed. François de Saint Just, a professional actor from Saint-Domingue, opened the theater and took over the troupe until it disbanded forever in 1810 due to a sheriff's closing. Other theaters took its place, including Le Petit Théâtre du Vieux Carré, a block farther down the street. Beginning in 1812, the property changed hands numerous times, to and from some of the most influential citizens in the city, including Attorney-General J. B. Labatut. A fire badly damaged the building in 1816. No drawings of the St. Peter Street theater have survived, but music historian Henry A. Kmen records the importance of the theater, which helped stage "at least three hundred fifty-one performances of seventy-six different operas. The works of thirty-two composers, the best in Europe, had been brought across the Atlantic and the Gulf. No other city in America and not too many in Europe could match this outpouring of opera." Most recently the property has been a pizzeria and a Greek restaurant.

Ghostly personages inhabit these historic places. In the Pat O'Brien's complex, employees say that in the early morning hours, they experience cold spots and eerie footsteps throughout the piano bar. A bartender, restocking the bar alone one afternoon, heard footsteps behind him going toward the piano, then the tinkling of piano keys. Alarmed that a trespasser had entered, he turned around quickly but saw no one. Other employees say the air stirs and turns chilly just before they are pushed by an unseen hand. The ladies' room on the second floor is haunted by a ghostly restroom attendant whose footsteps can be heard along with deep sighs and laughter from the stalls. Some women say that they experience uncontrollable apprehensiveness and anxiety as they approach the landing on the stairs to the ladies' room. Something, or someone, likes to move things around in the courtyard, even the heavy wrought-iron chairs and tables. During busy times this poltergeist will hide the green jackets that servers are supposed to wear, but employees say this ghost doesn't mean any harm. Another employee tells of a ghost resembling Ray Walston of the TV series *My Favorite Martian* who likes to have his photo taken in the courtyard.

In the small, austere, no-frills Preservation Hall, patrons are treated to authentic jazz under the leadership of Ben Jaffe, who grew up literally at the feet of legendary band members. Jazz greats play regularly well into their senior years. Many of those who have passed to the other side still hang around. Guests have described old ghosts playing trombones and saxophones. The creaky floor of the stage area indicates that they are in the building and ready to perform. Murky photographs of jazz legends seem to come to life as the music begins. In the old playhouse, little ghostly activity is reported today, but it is hard to keep tenants in the building. There certainly was trouble when the space was used as a theater, and in 1803 an official order was issued. In part, it stated,

> Article I: No person shall present himself to the several entrances of the theater without having a ticket of admittance, and if any be proven to have gained admission by cunning or otherwise or by having used violence, he will be brought before a competent magistrate . . .; Article II: The orchestra of the hall cannot be subject to fanciful demands to play this or that tune . . .; Article III: Neither shall anyone have the right of taking possession of a box or any place which shall have been rented to someone

else.; Article IV: No one shall express his approval or his disapproval in such a way as to disturb the calm of the theater, either by noisy clapping if pleased or hissing if displeased.; Article V: No one will be allowed to throw or to pretend to throw oranges or anything else, be it in the theater or in any part of the hall, nor in a word, shall anyone be allowed to start quarrels with his neighbor or with anyone. . . .

Perhaps the theatrical ghosts have moved down to Le Petit to attend performances in peace and quiet in the historic building just a block away.

Marcia blurted out her fantastic story. The girls had stopped at Preservation Hall to check out the performance times. Marcia was a concert violinist, and a trip to New Orleans meant music. When they looked at the notice on the window, they saw that the evening's performances had been canceled due to the funeral of one of the regular players. Marcia was saddened over the loss of yet another vintage New Orleans musician, but she was also disappointed that she would not be able to enjoy an evening of jazz. Then suddenly the wind kicked up and the temperature dropped, and when the girls looked again through the darkened window, before walking on, they saw some ancient musicians taking up their instruments. It was strange and eerie, Marcia explained; they had see-through bodies that swayed and twisted as they played saxophone, clarinet, bass, and trombone. She said she and Jill had stood in the doorway mesmerized by the ghostly concert. Passersby didn't seem to hear or see anything, and no staff was in sight. Jill was still ashen. "I had to pull Marcia away," she said. "You know how she loves that music!" The girls looked from one to the other, each one thinking, if this is the start of the weekend, what great adventures lay in store. "Well," Jill said, getting back to reality, "I think it's time for a drink and some dinner."

Chapter 14

Even Spirits
Like Irish Music

Many New Orleans streets and neighborhoods are quieter these days. In 2005 Hurricane Katrina's fierce winds and water surges upended many sections of the city, and though the French Quarter was spared the worst of her wrath, it was also one of her victims. Tourists canceled airline flights and hotel reservations. They avoided the city, wary of reliable transportation, restaurant availability, and openings and closings of business establishments. Above all, they didn't want to bear witness to the devastation that could be seen in the harrowed faces of city citizens. Katrina brought a halt to the nightly festivities and good times for many, especially those who favored the Celtic flavor of O'Flaherty's Irish Channel Pub. O'Flaherty's did not reopen its doors. The buildings, vacant now, have been bought by a group with plans to rebuild the area. Meanwhile, some of the most active ghosts in the French Quarter continue to inhabit the stilled premises in the 500 block of Toulouse Street.

Larry and Jay, junior architects in the firm, were charged with rechecking the specifications of the new plan for the building on Toulouse Street. The project manager didn't want any detail to be overlooked, nor any measurement, no matter how small or insignificant, to be wrong. It was important that the city council approve the plans at its meeting tomorrow. The two young men had checked and rechecked everything. Then Jay said offhandedly, "Maybe we should go to the site and look at the buildings firsthand. What if Mr. Lee missed something? We could, of course, grab lunch in the Quarter while we're there." Larry liked the idea; it would show the big bosses that, as serious young designers, they would leave no stone unturned. Besides, he was hungry. Larry and Jay headed out the office, walked briskly down St. Charles Avenue, and crossed over historic Canal Street.

It was a relatively cool day, with low humidity and scattered cloud cover. The French Quarter was alive during the extended lunch hours that prevailed in the "City That Care Forgot." Businessmen and women were scuttling across uneven walkways, dodging delivery vehicles and construction crews. Lunch was a serious business in New Orleans, and most locals had their favorite places to grab a bite—shrimp Creole, red beans and rice, blackened redfish, or crayfish étouffée. Larry was looking forward to a shrimp po'boy; Jay had his sights set on an overstuffed muffaletta. But first they had to visit the site, a complex of buildings in the 500 block of Toulouse Street that included the once popular O'Flaherty's.

The entrance was boarded up, but by prying loose the wooden planks that had been nailed across the front door, they were able to gain access. The building had been vacant since Hurricane Katrina. Larry had fond memories of evenings spent at O'Flaherty's, listening to Celtic music. The two men roamed through the buildings, stomped on the heavy wooden floor, and surveyed the overgrown courtyard. The plans seemed to be in order. Jay wanted to check out the large room on the third floor again and measure the windows one last time. Larry stayed near the pond, noticing that the fountain needed some renovation. He made a few notes to take back to the office. Then suddenly, without warning, a chilled air swept across his shoulders. Larry turned and saw a young woman standing near the fountain. How sad she looks, he thought, and then almost immediately, he wondered why she was wandering around an abandoned building. . . .

The buildings at 508 and 514 Toulouse Street in the French Quarter sit tightly about each other as if they are inseparable friends. And perhaps they are after two hundred years of sharing the same street and some of the same cast of characters.

From 1722 to 1802, when owner M. Bastien Estevan advertised the property for sale, 508 Toulouse had many owners. On March 3, 1803, Don Guillaume Marre bought the property, which included the ground-floor store (as was the custom during this time), two upper apartments, and an attic, and it was here that he brought his new bride, Mary Wheaton Sevre from New Jersey. Mary had already buried one husband, and this marriage didn't last long either. Marre died within three years, and Mary inherited the house. It was in this imposing brick building that a frightening tale took place.

At this time Joseph Baptandiere, a Frenchman from Hauteluce, Mont Blanc, was making his fortune in the feed and grain industry in New Orleans and was in the market for a wife. He was particularly attracted to Mary's Anglo-Saxon link to the "Americans" pouring into the area following the Louisiana Purchase a few years earlier, as well as her substantial inheritance. He was just starting out in his business, and the money, legitimacy, and connections her position offered him were sure to bring financial success. They were married in 1806. But it seems this was not a perfect union. Joseph found Americanization difficult and continued to hang on to his Old World ways. Like other Frenchmen he took part in plaçage, a practice by which Creole men, both married and single, took on and supported mistresses. A man was required by code to take care of his mistress, and she, in turn, was not to interfere with his public life or social obligations to his wife and family.

As Joseph's business thrived, he could afford to "keep" Angelique Dubois, one of the city's *demoiselles de couleur*. Some say she worked in his feed store and lived in an attic room above. How convenient. Of course, the truth could not get back to Mary, whose puritanical beliefs would not have approved of the arrangement.

Things went well for a while, it seems, and then the romance grew ugly. Not an overly attractive man, Joseph got fat, started balding, and became demanding, and Angelique grew difficult. She wanted more money, and more power— or she would tell his wife. In 1810, when Angelique began yet another argument, Joseph went into a fit of rage, grabbing at the young woman. She ran. He followed, huffing and puffing. When he caught up with her, he closed his hands tightly around her throat and began to choke the life out of her. Then he threw her unconscious body off the second-story balcony onto the courtyard below, breaking her neck. Joseph hurried down the stairs to cover up the crime. Thinking himself clever, he dropped Angelique's lifeless body into the reeking sewer that stood gaping in the courtyard. He might have gotten away with murder if it hadn't been for the young slave boy staring at him with wide, accusing eyes. The boy took off before Joseph could corner him. Fearing jail, execution, or worse—the shame he would bring to his family name—Joseph ran to the third floor, tied a rope around his neck, and jumped out the window. Mary had survived yet another husband, and she continued Joseph's business, living upstairs until her death in 1817.

In 1985, the building passed into the hands of Danny O'Flaherty, an Irishman with a flair for music and good times. He thought the historic, albeit haunted, building looked perfect for his Celtic music club. He also took over 514 Toulouse next door, a stucco building with an 1820 entresol level lit at floor level by the fan lights of the arched French door openings of the spacious commercial ground floor. O'Flaherty's complex, officially themed "Where Celtic Nations Meet," included a courtyard, ballard room, rowdy pub, restaurant, and Celtic gift shop. For twenty years ghosts had a splendid time mixing with patrons who enjoyed pints of Guinness and Irish music. The owner was aware of the ghostly spirits haunting his premises and laughed about the exorcist ritual that a disgruntled tour group operator had performed. The tour leader decided that, if he could not promenade through the bar unchecked, he would eliminate the ghosts, so competitors could not as well. The tour guide claimed he was successful and the ghosts had departed. But O'Flaherty later said on a television show, *Strange Universe,* that the ghosts were back. He quipped that they probably liked Celtic music or maybe it was the Irish stew. Customers eagerly attested to renewed sightings.

During the bar's best years, the ghosts of Joseph and Angelique were seen wandering through the upper floors of the building, especially near the window looking out on the balcony from which Angelique had been thrown. In the courtyard below a fountain gurgled into a pond near where the bodies had met their demise. Here customers reported "cold spots." A change in energy was also reported near the entrance to the upstairs bar. This presence was Angelique, a thin spirit with long hair who seemed sad and despondent. She would often reach out to touch young men and children with an icy hand. Her spirit was also seen moving slowly and sorrowfully around the third floor in the room from which Joseph hung himself. On her good days, Angelique seemed to enjoy the music and had a habit of appearing on the balcony to watch the activities downstairs in the Ballard Room. O'Flaherty sang "Red as a Rose" to her spirit, and many patrons reported her sudden appearance as he trilled the first note. She loved Danny's Irish flute and sighed longingly at his soulful ballads that recounted lost loves.

Joseph Baptandiere was not a kindly spirit. His murderous apparition grabbed at ghost hunters trying to document the haunting, leaving red depressions on their arms. One man reported an invisible rope tightening around his neck. After he managed to pull away, he discovered red rope burn marks on his neck. On the third floor where his family had lived, Joseph got aggressive, often pushing people down. An eerie echo pleading to be left alone could be heard resonating off the walls. His guilt-ridden and angry spirit didn't welcome visitors in this part of the building.

Mary's ghost was often seen standing near a second-story window, staring out as if she were still in shock. She was also seen on Friday nights in the restaurant and bar areas, where she seemed to come to life, checking up on the Celtic music and good food. Mary often roamed the premises to make sure everyone was behaving in a decorous manner; if people acted inappropriately, they would experience a slight shove from an unseen hand. Mary went into a snit when she saw attractive women, and when young women entered the Celtic Gift Shop at the rear of the courtyard, books would fly off the shelf.

Other spirits inhabited these buildings. Gruesome apparitions in a large room on the unused third floor were connected to yellow fever victims quarantined here during the 1853 epidemic. In this room, many people died and just as many jumped from the windows to end their misery on the hard, brick courtyard below. Iron bars were installed on the windows to stop the suicides, and they are still there today. Sadness, pain, and hopelessness permeate the room. Visitors reported lights flickering, doors inexplicably opening and closing, muffled coughing and sniffling, and extremely heavy, suffering-laden air near the windows.

After Katrina, a development company bought the 508–514 Toulouse Street property and announced renovation plans for a residential complex. Are the ghosts still here or did they evacuate with the living as hurricane winds and flood waters threatened the city?

Larry was confused as to how the woman had gotten into the courtyard. When he moved toward her, she disappeared without warning. Then he remembered the stories some of the guys around the office had been telling—tales of ghosts and eerie apparitions. The woman had seemed so real, yet he knew now she was not. Trying to clear his mind, he was startled when Jay bounded down the stairs as if being chased. "Larry, man, let's get out of here, fast," he yelled. "What's up?" Larry asked. "I just saw a ghost—a real ghost," Jay continued breathlessly. "A man standing by the window where I was measuring suddenly had his hands on my throat. I had to fight him off—didn't you hear anything?" Larry thought he would have some fun with his colleague. "Ghosts, really?" Larry laughed. "You don't believe in all that stuff, do you? That's for kooks." "No, man," Jay gasped, "really, it was a ghost!" Larry would keep his own ghost sighting to himself and continue the jabs. "Hey, Jay, do you think we should put your ghost in our report to the boss?"

Chapter 15
A Pirate's Prize

Brothers Pierre and Jean Lafitte built a lucrative pirate and priva-teering business in Barataria, a low, marshy area south of New Orleans. At its heyday, the Lafitte enterprise included more than one thousand Baratarians and roughly one hundred ships. Pierre and Jean were major figures in New Orleans, supposedly operating a blacksmith shop where they passed absconded goods to agents and citizens in the city. Jean Lafitte was instrumental in helping Andrew Jackson fight off the British in the Battle of New Orleans in 1815. When the war was over and the brothers continued to hijack ships and disobey custom laws, Louisiana Governor William C. C. Claiborne offered a $500 reward for their capture. The brazen Lafittes responded with posters offering a $1,500 reward for the delivery of the governor to Barataria.

Ryan loved his job. Each evening as he dressed for work, he felt his heart sing. He would put the day's worries behind him and look forward to entering the careless, beguiling world that awaited him at Lafitte's Blacksmith Shop, a small French Quarter bar, on the corner of Bourbon and St. Phillip Streets. Many of his friends had "regular" jobs, and though they could not hang out with him during the day, he was sure to see some of them most every evening at Lafitte's. But tonight was different. It was his birthday, and he knew there would be a party for him before the night was over. He made a mental note to keep his eyes and ears open— "special" persons often appeared in the bar when big parties were happening. Ryan arrived at Lafitte's ready for his 6 p.m. to 2 a.m. shift. All was calm. Several patrons were already nursing drinks at the bar, trying to wash away the day's stress, disappointment, or fear. Ryan knew each person had a story to tell. He was glad not only to serve drinks but also to listen to the customers' tales of woe, love gone wrong or right, or expectant hopes for the future.

"Happy Birthday." The whisper was faint; in fact, he wondered if he had heard the words only in his head. Ryan looked toward the still-dark back room of the establishment. Only later would patrons, drinks in hand, make their way to that area. The shadowy form contracted upon itself, and in a split second, Jean Lafitte, buccaneer of old, appeared. The pirate known to appreciate a "good time" had come for his party. The man's good looks made him easily distinguishable from his pirate cohorts who were also present. Ryan looked forward to engaging Lafitte's sophisticated wit and gentlemanly manner if only for a few minutes before the rest of his party friends arrived. Knowing the visitor who made rare appearances had come for his birthday celebration was a great start for the rest of the evening. Ryan poured drinks for all the spirits, and they exchanged a few knowing glances. Then Ryan looked up and saw a buddy of his coming in the front door. . . .

Jean Lafitte, the youngest of eight siblings, was about twenty-six years old when he came to New Orleans as a blacksmith around 1806, or perhaps a few years earlier or later. It is said that his father was either a *forgeron*, a blacksmith specializing in wrought iron, in France and Jean was to follow in his footsteps or his father was a skilled leatherworker who had emigrated from France to the Caribbean, where he made his fortune. Some records say Jean Lafitte was born in Marseilles, a seaport in the south of France. Other sources report his birth in Port-au-Prince, Saint-Domingue, now Haiti. At least one source says he came to New Orleans with government letters granting him a license to operate as a privateer. His early history is murky. It seems Lafitte often made up and reinvented the facts of his personal and professional lives to both impress customers and confuse government officials. Records do show that by 1808 or so, brothers Pierre, older by two years, and Jean had established a lucrative, though perhaps nefarious, business as smugglers and slave importers in Barataria, a low-lying area south of New Orleans encircling Barataria Bay. The brothers led a band of cutthroats who attacked anything that floated and used the small blacksmith shop on Bourbon Street to disperse the plunder—liquor, weapons, gold, and slaves—throughout the area and up the Mississippi River to other ports.

The two men were destined to become part of Louisiana's checkered past, though Jean Lafitte would prove to be the most notorious and most mysterious. As dashing French pirates, property and slave owners, businessmen, slave smugglers, thieves, kidnappers, drug dealers, and perhaps murderers, they made their mark in the early annals of New Orleans history. The brothers were engaged in both legal and illegal trade. As privateers they received letters of marque from the French government in Martinique and Guadalupe, which allowed them to capture enemy ships for the authorities. They also became actively engaged in the pirate trade, preying upon Spanish ships navigating the Gulf of Mexico south of New Orleans. The brothers used their network to illegally import slaves, a practice that was banned in the United States in 1808.

The old structure at 941 Bourbon Street that was to become Lafitte's Blacksmith Shop was built in the late 1700s in the French Colonial Louis XV *briquette-entre-poteaux* (brick between posts) construction, a technique imported from Haiti, a French colony. It is one of the oldest buildings in New Orleans, a remnant of the city's French past, and it proudly displays its Louisiana-made mud bricks. The cottage was flush with the street, and a garden profuse with oleander and date-palms was shielded from the busy street by a high wall. Business was conducted in the downstairs rooms; the living quarters were upstairs.

Much of the iron grillwork and balconies of the early Spanish architecture, which replaced the French structures in the city after the devastating fires of 1788 and 1794, were supposedly crafted in the Lafitte brothers' shop by slaves. Some say the Lafittes supplied churches, wealthy citizens, and government officials with beautiful iron grilles, railings, and fences in exchange for under-the-table promises not to interfere with their illegal trade and business operations. Others say no blacksmith work ever took place in the building and the shop was merely a facade for the lucrative trade of slave smuggling and piracy.

The early 1800s were a lucrative time for the Lafittes. Their trade was booming, and they frequented the best homes and establishments in the city. They were guests and business partners of noted gentlemen. Jean Lafitte could speak several languages: French, Spanish, English, and Italian. The brothers attended quadroon balls, played poker, drank, and partied into the early hours of the morning in ruffled shirts and tight-fitting suits.

Eventually, though, the government shut down the Lafitte operation, and the brothers were arrested, along with their men. The War of 1812 was in full swing by this time, and while Jean was out on bail, he was contacted by British officers who offered him the rank of captain and protection for his buccaneering enterprises if he would join with them against the United States. Lafitte silently rejected the British offer but pretended to accept. Facing a jail sentence, and hoping to get his brother freed, Jean informed Governor Claiborne of the British offer and pledged to help defend New Orleans if a deal could be worked out for himself, his brother Pierre, and his men. Andrew Jackson was said to have met with Jean Lafitte to plan the battle against the English as they neared New Orleans's port. After fighting bravely in the Battle of New Orleans, Jean Lafitte was hailed as a patriotic citizen of the city and proclaimed a hero. President James Madison pardoned the Lafitte brothers and their men on February 6, 1815. But instead of reforming and becoming law-abiding citizens, Jean and Pierre continued their buccaneering.

Business was brisk back at the blacksmith shop, at least the job of camouflaging the movement of contraband was. Governments of every seafaring nation gave Jean the moniker "Terror of the Gulf." As officials began to crack down on the Lafittes, Jean moved on to found the city of Galveston as his home base. He is said to have eventually moved to Cuba, angering Cuban officials by robbing incoming Spanish ships of needed supplies. When Colombia in South America began hiring privateers, Jean Lafitte joined up and was part of a government-run plan to rob Spanish ships. Some say he died in a fierce battle with a merchant ship, or perhaps it was yellow fever that ended his life in 1826. Others say he returned to die in his beloved Louisiana, where some of his men had achieved celebrity status.

Tales of confiscated wealth and priceless hidden treasures swirl around the Lafitte brothers. Many believers say some booty is still hidden within the walls of the former blacksmith shop, and numerous spirits float in and around the place, trying to find it. Some ghosts arrive on horseback, others come and go as temporary treasure hunters, and a few spirits are forever connected to the shop and remain permanent residents. Ghost lore says that when a pirate buries a treasure, he kills someone on the spot. That person's spirit is then a ghost slave and eternal guard of the treasure, allowing no one other than the person who hid the treasure to unearth it. The fireplace in the downstairs bar is rumored to hold a cache of Lafitte's personal gold, but it is said to be haunted by the ghost of the pirate Lafitte killed to protect the treasure for eternity. However, it seems Jean Lafitte died without retrieving all his treasure, and so his cursed spirit roams the blacksmith shop . . . waiting.

Legend has it that the ghosts will be released to pass from this world to the next only when a pure heart finds the treasure that had been hidden with human blood and puts the goods to noble use. Many stories revolve around the fireplace, the most likely spot for hidden treasure to be buried. In this area the air is extremely chilly and patrons of the bar as well as staff members report seeing flaming ghostly eyes, dripping with blood, through the fireplace grate. The eyes seem to stare right at them. Others see long, pointy, beckoning fingers. Perhaps Lafitte is trying to show those with pure hearts where the treasure is hidden. Believers of tall tales say that, although the buried treasure may be deep under the ancient brick fireplace, it will never be found because of all the cursing, spitting, and drinking that goes on in the bar. Folklore says that pirate's gold sinks lower into the ground when surrounded by despicable characters and goings-on. If that's the case, the treasure is well out of reach and halfway to China by now.

Several witnesses have reported seeing Jean Lafitte's tall ghost with pale skin and deep, dark eyes looking out from the dark recesses of the bar, twisting his black mustache in his gloved hand, as if overseeing yet another grand plot to acquire gold or slaves. The pungent aroma of a lit cigar can be detected when Lafitte's spirit lifts a drink in salute at a table behind the piano bar. Those who sit at tables near the fireplace say Lafitte's specter physically reaches out to them when he wants their attention and describe the touch of a cold, ghostly hand. Others report that as soon as they become aware of the man's presence, he vanishes, much as he did in history. No one knows for sure where or how he died . . . or even if he did.

Most ghosts that frequent Lafitte's Blacksmith Shop just want to relax and throw back a brew. Happy patrons return looking for camaraderie and take pleasure in mingling with the guests as they used to back in the day. A short, pudgy spirit has been seen walking out of the fireplace, sauntering to the end of the bar, and then simply disappearing. A mirror upstairs is haunted by the specter of a woman from a much earlier time. No one knows who she is. People are not the only haunts frequenting the bar. A ghostly image of a horse bending down as if to drink from a trough has also been sighted in front of the shop.

There are no electric lights in Lafitte's Blacksmith Shop bar, as only flickering candles illuminate the dark-wooded interior. A decrepit courtyard oozes with unearthly ambience. It's easy to imagine that the spirit of Jean Lafitte is still overseeing his ghostly pirate empire. The old building looks as if it could collapse at any moment; a few wooden beams appear to offer little stability.

But there is a lot of life yet to be had in the old New Orleans establishment, in this life and the next. In 1970 Lafitte's Blacksmith Shop was certified as a National Historic Landmark. The bar is said to be the oldest continually occupied bar in the United States.

Ryan raised a hand to say hello to his friend walking into the bar . . . and then Jean Lafitte and his infamous band of pirates faded into walls that had been standing for more than two centuries. Ryan signaled to the woman at the old piano that it was time to start the entertainment. He knew his visit with the Lafitte gang had come to an end. It was time to mix up a batch of "Voodoo Daiquiris," the grape-flavored slushy drink beloved by Lafitte's patrons, and start his birthday party. More friends waved as they came into the cool interior from the sweltering heat and humidity that was truly New Orleans. They raised their hands to signal for him to start pouring their drinks.

Chapter 16

The Old Absinthe
House Lives the Past

One of the oldest structures in the French Quarter, the Old Absinthe House, has seen its share of history. It has housed a thriving import business, served as a local grocery store and cafe, and provided dapper Creole gentlemen with a quiet place to sip their absinthe, protected from the hustle and bustle of noisy city streets. The upstairs secret room reportedly hosted talks between General Andrew Jackson and pirate Jean Lafitte, as they planned the defense of New Orleans against the British in 1814. This iconic building has been at the center of the city's commercial life for more than two hundred years. Today, no trip to New Orleans is complete without a stop at the Old Absinthe House, where guests order Herbsaint absinthe, reflect on a bygone era, and toast the many old ghosts haunting this picturesque locale.

Liz and Jeff were visiting New Orleans, the "City That Care Forgot," again. They came back once a year but never seemed to do everything they planned. Spontaneity usually ruled their vacations, but today they had a definite goal. They would enjoy a drink or two at the Old Absinthe House at 240 Bourbon Street, so they could check that off their to-do list. The summer day was extremely hot and steamy . . . sweltering, in fact. As they approached the corner of Bienville and Bourbon Streets, the couple quickened their steps. They were looking forward to wallowing in the cool air inside the bar, hoping that once the sun went down, the cobbled streets would seem more inviting and they could walk around the French Quarter a little more. True to their mission they located the flat Spanish Colonial brick building with the fanlight transoms hugging the street. Sitting at the long, coppery bar, large enough to accommodate fifty patrons, they both ordered an Absinthe House Frappe, the bar's signature drink. It tasted so refreshing and sweet . . . and strong. They were still looking around at the antique chandeliers and exposed cypress beams when they ordered their second round.

Feeling at ease in the old place, Liz reached for her glass and another sip of the stimulating concoction. But where was her drink? It was on the other side of Jeff. Strange that he should move it, she thought. Then she noticed that some of the glass bottles that had been on the shelf behind the bar were now lined up near her right elbow. How peculiar, she thought, but she was not in the mood to be perturbed. The afternoon was finally coming to a close, and the heat was abating. Liz heard chairs moving rhythmically back and forth as if a large group was taking up seats for happy hour. She turned around to see who had ventured into the place. Maybe that was why Robert, the bartender, had put the liquor bottles next to her. But she saw no one pulling out chairs from the tables; Jeff was silently sipping his drink and swaying to the jukebox as if he had heard nothing. Liz motioned to Robert; she needed answers. "Why did you put these bottles here?" she asked, pointing to her right. The bartender blinked slightly. "Oh, I didn't put those bottles there—you will have to ask the spirits why they did that." He smiled down at Liz as he rearranged the bottles a little nervously. "Perhaps a ghostly party has arrived to enjoy the evening," he said. "Want to join them?"

The Old Absinthe House is a grand old New Orleans tavern that has played a prominent role in Vieux Carré life for more than two hundred years. Spanish brothers Pedro Font and Francisco Juncadella bought the site in 1806 and the next year built the two-story entresol building with a curved wrought-iron balcony. The brothers used the downstairs space as their importing firm's headquarters and an establishment that was much like a neighborhood grocery store and cafe, trading and bartering food, tobacco, and Spanish liquor. The second story was used as a residence. It seems the pirate Jean Lafitte befriended the brothers and conducted some of his buccaneering business out of their establishment. Tunnels carved out under the building may have been used to move illegal goods in and out of the city. It is said that Lafitte felt so safe here among his friends that in 1814 he agreed to meet General Andrew Jackson in a private upstairs room. Though Lafitte was often on the wrong side of the law, the two men climbed the back staircase together, to work out a crucial plan to defeat the British in the Battle of New Orleans. The staircase, constructed using wooden pegs, is still there—a testament to the longevity of the historical building. Lafitte and his one thousand-man brigade fought heroically during the Battle of New Orleans, raising Lafitte to local hero status. It seems that Jean Lafitte's ghost has decided to remain among his close friends from these early days. And, if legend is to be believed, after the bar closes and the doors are locked, employees have seen the ghosts of Jackson and Lafitte slowly climb up the old staircase to strategize once again about saving the city.

After Font's return to Spain and Juncadella's death, the ground floor continued to serve as a retail grocery store. It briefly operated as a boot store in the 1830s, but by the 1840s, the ground floor was once again a grocery store, which morphed into a popular tavern known as Aleix's Coffee House, run by Jacinto Aleix and his brother, nephews of the widow of Juncadella. "Coffee houses" sold alcoholic refreshments, including absinthe, a popular European spirit high in alcohol volume. "Absynthe" appeared in New Orleans ads as early as 1837, but it wasn't until 1870 that its popularity soared. Aleix's Coffee House hired the Barcelona Spaniard Cayetano Ferrer, who had made a name for himself as the chief mixologist at the French Opera House basement bar. Ferrer created the signature Absinthe House Frappe and served it in the Parisian manner with marble fountains dripping cold water onto lumps of sugar suspended on perforated spoons over glasses of absinthe. The drink was so acclaimed that the tavern was renamed the Absinthe Room in 1874 and twenty years later was rechristened by Ferrer's sons, now in the business, as the Old Absinthe House. The special copper-colored bar, water-dripper spigot, and antique fixtures appealed aesthetically to New Orleans salon society, and patrons of Creole balls, the Théâtre d'Orleans, and the French Opera House. History notes that when Edgar Degas and Oscar Wilde spent part of the 1800s in French-speaking New Orleans, they had no trouble finding imported French absinthes.

But the good times were soon to come to an end. Because absinthe was reputed to cause hallucinations, blindness, delirium, madness, and even death, it was banned in the United States and most of Europe in 1912. Substitutes for the wormwood herb used to make the original concoction were offered, but a preference for the "new" drink was not realized. The coffeehouse operated as a speakeasy during Prohibition, but federal officers, alerted to its illegal business, eventually closed the doors of the Old Absinthe House in 1924. Faced with threats by temperance supporters to burn the bar to the ground, the owners quickly moved their prized copper-colored wooden bar and other valuable furnishings to a warehouse in New Orleans. The bar reopened after Prohibition, and in 2004, after a million-dollar renovation, the original bar top was returned to the Old Absinthe House.

One of the oldest ghosts residing in the Old Absinthe House is Jean Lafitte. Young and slim with a grand, curved mustache, wearing his signature pirate hat, tight blue pants, and red sash, he roams the premises from early evening into the night. He often appears to bar patrons, approaches them as if to start up a conversation, and then suddenly vanishes. Lafitte's specter prefers to visit the second-floor meeting room where he plotted with Andrew Jackson, but he is also seen downstairs drinking and laughing with friends and long-departed pirates as he moves from table to table. These spirit parties get rowdy at times. Employees report chairs and dishes moving on their own and things flying off the walls. Many ghostly entities of no special importance return to the Old Absinthe House to relive the good times they once spent here. Parties are frequent, bottles of liquor are dispensed, and glasses are raised in salute to better days. Strange noises can be traced to the vicinity of the legendary underground tunnels. Many insist that the tunnels, one connected to Lafitte's Blacksmith Shop farther down Bourbon Street, also link up with the Old US Mint on Esplanade Avenue. Patrons have witnessed flitting shadows escaping into the darkness; perhaps surreptitious trade deals are still being transacted.

Other ghostly sightings include a phantom woman and a lost child accompanied by unexplained power outages and cool breezes wafting through the bar. Imbibers have described being touched and pinched by unseen presences; some report spirits who tug on their clothes and hair. Even famous guest phantoms have visited the infamous tavern. Locals and staff have chronicled seeing New Orleans composer Louis Moreau Gottschalk, the feared Benjamin Butler, and Voodoo Queen Marie Laveau. Noted frequenters of the Old Absinthe House, such as P. T. Barnum, William Thackeray, Walt Whitman, Mark Twain, Aaron Burr, and Frank Sinatra may be among the nightly revelers. They have all enjoyed a drink here supporting the bar's predictive motto: Everyone you have known or ever will know eventually ends up at the Old Absinthe House.

A revival of drinking absinthe began in the 1990s; the European Union reauthorized its manufacture and sale. In the United States use of the original absinthe ingredient, the wormwood plant, is still banned. In New Orleans, the Herbsaint, a potent, locally made anise liquor, is used for the Absinthe Frappe. It is said to rival the best absinthe in the world. Today, the front first-floor room of the Spanish Colonial town home is still the Old Absinthe House with its decorative marble fountain and brass faucets used to drip cool water over sugar cubes into glasses of absinthe. The historical building also houses Tony Moran's Restaurant in the rear downstairs and the Jean Lafitte Bistro upstairs.

Liz reached across the bar over her husband's hands that were cradling his drink and pulled her frappe in front of her. As she slowly sipped the beguiling green liquid, referred to as *la fée verte* (the green fairy), she heard her favorite song coming from the jukebox in the bar. It seemed so apropos for their visit to the Old Absinthe House. "Can you play Sinatra's 'That's Life' for me, again?" she asked her husband. Jeff sauntered over to the music box and searched for the title his wife had requested. She heard a door open, then close, but when she looked around, no one had come in or gone out. Everything was still the same, almost as if frozen in time. Liz smiled secretly to herself. "It's not on the jukebox list at all," Jeff relayed back. "You couldn't have heard the song, Liz." "Hmm," Liz said, "I certainly did hear it."

Chapter 17

The Commander is Still at the Helm

Emile Commander opened his restaurant in 1880 to give grieving friends and family a place to rest and enjoy comforting Creole food before and after visits to the grave sites of loved ones in Lafayette Cemetery No. 1, across the street. Commander's Palace became one of the premier restaurants in New Orleans, attracting visitors from around the world. Emile, himself, took personal pride in building a loyal local clientele, and he has hung around for more than a century to welcome his guests and make sure his high standards are precisely maintained.

Ellie was excited about her nephew's upcoming marriage to Jessica, a lovely Southern girl from St. Amant, a small town just outside Baton Rouge. She had persuaded the couple to hold their engagement dinner at Commander's Palace in the heart of the Garden District and had helped with all the planning. Ellie was a New Orleans woman, born and raised, and she wanted her nephew, Christian, to share her love of the city's traditions, especially the fine dining establishments. Early on the evening of the celebration, Ellie took the St. Charles streetcar to Washington Avenue, then walked one block toward the Mississippi River. She always smiled when the large turquoise and white turreted Victorian clapboard house popped into view. Following the aromatic smells wafting from the busy kitchen, her feet nearly floated to the door of Commander's Palace. Ellie met with the manager, who indicated with an extended arm where the engagement dinner was set up. Ellie needed no tour guide; she was already headed to the stunning sun porch at the rear of the restaurant, her favorite spot whenever she came to lunch or dinner. She looked at the sparkling wine bottle already opened to breathe.

She had selected the famous turtle soup for starters, yes, of course, with a touch of sherry. She smiled, knowing she was part of an inner circle of gourmands who knew what to order at which famous restaurant in the city. The main course would be skillet-seared Gulf fish with spicy crab-boiled veggies. The manager left her alone on the sun porch to tend to another party, and Ellie reached to the table and poured a small amount of wine in a glass to test it. She certainly didn't want less than perfect wine to spoil the evening ahead. Taking a small sip, she stood looking out over the courtyard, eagerly anticipating the first guests to arrive, but she knew she was not waiting alone. Ellie turned quickly to her left and raised one eyebrow as she felt a shadowy presence darting here, then there. She knew it was Emile Commander. In fact, she always looked forward to his wink and nod whenever she visited, no worry that Emile was the restaurant's founder and resident ghost for more than a hundred years. When Ellie reached for the wine bottle to set it back in the center of the table, it was empty. "Emile, now you just stop that," she whispered, before calling the manager over to discuss the problem.

The French Quarter's Vieux Carré is the oldest section of New Orleans. Throughout the eighteenth century it was inhabited by the Spanish, French, and Creoles who lived, worked, and fought under various European sovereignties. When the United States annexed the area granted by the Louisiana Purchase in 1803, Americans poured into the city, eager to make their fortunes in the growing commercial trades made even more inviting by the proximity to the Mississippi River and the Gulf of Mexico. But New Orleanians did not welcome these nineteenth-century American "foreigners." They were viewed as newcomers and usurpers. The Americans themselves felt like foreigners in a strange city where residents spoke French, Spanish, or a combination of these languages and very little English. To settle in New Orleans meant they had to forge out new territory for their homes and neighborhoods away from the Creole-dominated system of society and politics. The "Yankees" settled in an area upriver from the French Quarter that was designed in 1832 and officially christened the City of Lafayette in 1834. Cotton agents, bankers, and exporters quickly became wealthy, and their homes reflected their fortunes. Lafayette was annexed in 1852 as the fourth district of New Orleans, and the area had already earned the moniker "the Garden District" because of it spacious lots and exquisite flora. The Garden District, as this area is still known today, is home to some of the most stately houses in the country. The Classic Revival architecture breathes extravagance and opulence; renowned architects Henry Howard, Lewis E. Reynolds, and William Freret designed distinctive homes for wealthy citizens.

The Garden District was a favorite spot for many illustrious figures visiting the city. In *Life on the Mississippi*, Mark Twain immortalized the area in loving terms: "These mansions stand in the center of large grounds, and rise, garlanded with roses, out of the midst of swelling masses of shining green foliage and many-colored blossoms. No houses could well be in better harmony with their surroundings, or more pleasing to the eye, or more home-like and comfortable-looking." By the 1860s New Orleans boasted the largest cotton market in the world, and coupled with other growing trades, New Orleans was the wealthiest city in the nation. Residential and business districts enjoyed unprecedented growth. But its success as a bustling commercial center was soon to be the downfall for New Orleans. The Civil War was looming. Louisiana officially seceded from the Union on January 26, 1861, and a year later the city, its port, and all river trade were controlled by Union troops. The occupation would last fifteen years.

As the Reconstruction period ended, people returned to ordinary life and their business enterprises. This was a boom time for local businesses, and Emile Commander was quick to take advantage of the good times. Emile opened his restaurant at 1403 Washington Avenue at the corner of Coliseum Street in the Garden District to cater to the rich merchants and wealthy families who were calling this area their home. The site he chose, part of the former Livaudais Plantation, across from Lafayette Cemetery No. 1, seemed filled with promise. The cemetery had been laid out by Benjamin Buisson in 1833, and when New Orleans annexed the City of Lafayette in 1852, the graveyard became the first planned cemetery in New Orleans. Buisson was one of Napoleon's exiled lieutenants who became surveyor of Lafayette and named one of the area's main thoroughfares Napoleon Avenue; other street names reflected Napoleon's military victories.

Commander's Palace, as Emile called his large Victorian eating establishment, appealed to the "up and coming" and served the finest cuisine of the day in an atmosphere of utmost respectability. Emile did not offer the traditional French cuisine that most diners were used to and that made his place even more unique. The Americans, often shunned and mocked by the old French families of the city, wanted to eat at Commander's Palace simply because it did not offer French fare.

By the 1920s, Commander's Palace was under different management, but it continued to offer elegant dining in beautiful surroundings. The downstairs dining room was a favorite of the Garden District social set. However, this was not the only face of Commander's Palace. The Roaring Twenties were in full swing, and many illegal activities were sought out by those who could afford them. Most of the restaurant's second-floor rooms were reserved for gambling and drinking. Others rooms upstairs were designated meeting places for wealthy gentlemen and their painted mistresses. Riverboat captains and other less respectable guests frequenting the establishment could enter through a separate entrance and entertain in the private dining rooms upstairs out of sight of the well-to-do families dining below.

Prohibition laws were repealed in 1933, and the private quarters and secluded dining rooms upstairs were no longer needed. Commander's Palace relied on its long-standing respectable reputation secured by the downstairs family dining rooms, and guests looking for a singular culinary experience once again filled the tables on both floors.

In 1944, Frank and Elinor Moran bought the restaurant and renovated the building. They also expanded the menu to include more modern-day recipes, some of which continue to be offered today. By 1969, Commander's Palace found its way into the Brennan family of New Orleans eateries, and again its interior was redesigned and modernized. Large windows that overlooked the inner courtyard enhanced the view of diners, trellises accommodated lush climbing flowers, and original paintings were commissioned. It was just after this extensive renovation that the spirit of Emile Commander increased his activity. Perhaps he was unhappy with the changes to his life's work, or maybe he just wanted to be a part of the new tradition of excellence that continues into the twenty-first century. Since the renovation, silverware and dishes are often found changed around or missing altogether. Staff members report that lights turn on and off for no explicable reason, and there is talk of footsteps heard roaming the restaurant late at night after guests have gone home. All agree that the ghostly spirit is likable, though he frequently causes trouble by sipping from the drinks of guests, sometimes draining the glass entirely. Waiters don't bat an eyelid when guests complain that their wine somehow disappeared; they just grab another bottle from the wine cellar and pour some more.

Commander's Palace has a long history of culinary excellence and has been the home to some famous chefs. In 1975, Paul Prudhomme, renowned father of blackened redfish, became the first American-born executive chef of the restaurant. He created Louisiana fusion cuisine and introduced the new category of American cooking to the world. In 1982 Emeril Lagasse, the television chef, replaced Prudhomme and began to "spice it up," becoming well-known for his culinary innovations.

The modern Commander's Palace (when locals call the 130-year-old restaurant simply Commander's, everyone knows what they are talking about) has won awards from the James Beard Foundation, *Wine Spectator* magazine, and the Culinary Institute of America. The haute Creole dishes are the pride of what the present chef calls "dirt to plate within one hundred miles" freshness. First cousins Ti Adelaide Martin and Lally Brennan are managing the restaurant today. New Orleanians treasure the restaurant, and today's Garden District is a dynamic community proud of its strong sense of tradition. Some homes are still known by family names more than a century old.

When the dinner was over, and the favorite dessert, bread pudding soufflé, devoured, Ellie stood up to toast the young couple. The sated guests raised full wine glasses; Ellie had made sure of that detail. Yes, Emile Commander was still there enjoying the celebration. In Katrina's wake, the kitchen has been restored with state-of-the-art equipment, and most of the restaurant has new interior walls, stripped down to bare wooden studs. But miraculously this room had escaped extensive water damage and needed little renovation. Perhaps that is why the old man feels so comfortable here. He certainly visits quite often. Ellie said her goodnights to the guests and glanced in Emile's direction as she longingly departed the gracious restaurant where time seemed to stand still for an evening.

Chapter 18

Spirits Have
Royal Titles, Too

Tourists flock to New Orleans to enjoy a meal or two at some of the most legendary eateries in the country, but Arnaud's restaurant holds a special place in the hearts of true-blooded New Orleanians. Like the city herself, Arnaud's has been through highs and lows, good times and bad. Its comfortable setting attracts those who want to celebrate the milestones of their lives in a unique Crescent City ambience. Its on-site Mardi Gras museum displaying ethereal ball gowns, rhinestone tiaras, and bejeweled scepters reminds diners of how good life can be. Of course, everyone knows there are ghosts here. They are part of the old building so rich in history and vibrantly connected to the people who stop for a fleeting moment to cherish all that Arnaud's has to offer.

Dan and Gloria had been married for fifty years, and more than forty anniversary dinners had been celebrated at Arnaud's restaurant in the French Quarter. They fell in love with Arnaud's as a honeymooning couple, had dubbed it "their" place, and regretted the years they had canceled anniversary reservations because of sick children, out-of-town functions, or conflicts in busy schedules. The couple knew the history of the restaurant by heart. When it changed hands in 1978, the new owner became a dear friend who treated them to a complimentary glass of wine each year.

Gloria was looking forward to her night out. A tough winter was still hanging on despite the calendar. March had certainly come in like a lion. The couple visited the Mardi Gras museum, "oohing" over mannequins dressed in Germaine's French-made ball gowns. Then Josh, an apprentice waiter, showed the couple to their favorite table. They ordered dinner: Shrimp Ravigote appetizer, Gulf Fish Courtbouillon, and Veal Tenderloin Meunière. They would save room for dessert of Café Brûlot. Gloria began to look around the room, as if searching for something or someone. . . . She glanced up at the mezzanine, furrowing her brow, and looked toward the beveled glass windows. A smile crossed her lips, and she felt at ease. The old Count was here; of course, he wouldn't miss their anniversary. What had she been thinking? But tonight was different. Tonight she needed the Count. She had something to tell Dan, and she needed support. Gloria motioned to the Count hovering over the busboy who had just dropped a plate and beckoned him over to the table. He walked straight toward her. . . .

By the close of the nineteenth century, New Orleans was a hustling metropolis. The New Orleans Mint had reopened in 1879, and the 1884 World's Fair had put New Orleans on the map as an original place to visit. Electric lights came on in 1886, and electric streetcars replaced mule-drawn trolleys. By the dawn of the twentieth century, New Orleans had changed from a quaint French town to a modern American city. English became the language of business and commerce. Modern science eradicated the yellow fever epidemics that had plagued the city. Major storms in 1909 and 1915 brought destruction but also funds for "modernization" efforts in an old city in need of repair. In 1917, Storyville's red light district was closed. Amusement parks were set up along Lake Pontchartrain for family entertainment, and jazz clubs sprang up as the musical style of Louis Armstrong grew in popularity.

In this active social scene, a legendary restaurant was born. Frenchman Leon Bertrand Arnaud Cazenave headed to the United States to study medicine after finishing at the Lycée Napoleon in Paris and marrying Lady Irma Lamothe. Thwarted by money and time, he decided medicine was not for him. Instead he put his knowledge of French wines to good use and by 1918 was working in the Crescent City as a wine and champagne salesman. But the colorful entrepreneur had bigger aspirations than hawking spirits. His dreams were realized when he bought an old warehouse on Bienville Street and opened Arnaud's restaurant. He brazenly hired a female chef; Madame Pierre was a woman with extraordinary Creole cuisine skills. Arnaud's kitchen produced Shrimp Arnaud, Oysters Bienville, praline crepes, and a sauce bottled and sold as the "Original Creole Remoulade." Cazenave's flamboyant nature was infused into the very essence of his restaurant. He was known for sipping champagne every morning for breakfast and for carousing late into the night. Though he was not nobility, he commandeered the title of "Count."

Count Cazenave knew his patrons often wanted privacy. A mezzanine floor along the back wall above the main dining room allowed for romantic seclusion. The Count could also use this lookout to discreetly oversee what was going on in the dining room below. He provided his Richelieu Bar customers with a private street entrance and exit. Just inside the door sat a wooden "stoopie bench," where overexuberant imbibers could take a short nap before leaving. The Count opened the "gentlemen only" French 75 Bar, naming it after the French 75 mm cannon of World War I. The French 75 cocktail, a potent mixture of cognac, lemon juice, syrup, and champagne is almost as lethal. During Prohibition, the Count served liquor as "coffee" and it flowed freely in the private rooms. He substituted the more pedestrian gin for cognac in the French 75 and served the beverage in a coffee cup. Nevertheless, the law caught up with the Count, and the restaurant was padlocked for a time.

Committed to fine dining in a lavish setting, Cazenave commissioned distinctive silver, glassware, and china patterns, and laid out an intricate floor design of small Italian tiles that subtly changed colors and patterns from room to room. Buzzers were installed to summon waiters to locked dining rooms, and these are still working today. After World War II, Arnaud's became even more popular, as New Orleans replaced a destroyed Europe as a destination choice.

Unfortunately, the Count's health declined; he died in 1948, and his adoring and adored daughter, Germaine, took over as his successor. Germaine was given to extremes of drinking and celebrating like her father, and though many doubted her ability to run the restaurant, she was determined to maintain her father's legacy. She learned the business quickly. Known simply as "Germaine," she was one-of-a-kind in a city full of unusual characters. She loved the royal rituals of Mardi Gras and reigned as queen of twenty-two opulent carnival balls from 1937 to 1968, a record unlikely ever to be broken. Wanting to show off her posh and plentiful hats, she began the city's now-traditional Easter parade, replete with colorful bonnets and horse-drawn buggies. Her flair and flamboyant style garnered newspaper attention, and she managed to get Arnaud's on the elite restaurant lists of Paris and New York.

In 1978 Germaine viewed her approaching retirement not as giving up the family business, but as abdicating her throne. Following her father's lead, she handpicked her successor, choosing Archie Casbarian to continue Arnaud's legacy. Her decision was based on her peculiar sense of drama: Archie Casbarian had the same initials as her father, both men loved good cigars and cognac and could tell an amusing story, both were born overseas and spoke fluent French, they were about the same height, and they resembled each other in good looks.

Casbarian, an Egyptian, had attended hotel school in Switzerland and New York. In New Orleans he managed the Royal Sonesta hotel across the street from Arnaud's. Here he made the fateful acquaintance of Germaine.

Casbarian, determined to modernize the aging Arnaud's, began extensive renovations, and that meant closing the dining rooms for a while. To appease Arnaud's loyal supporters, he provided keys to the private street entrance of the Richelieu Bar, which would remain open throughout the renovations. They could relax at the bar and watch the construction process. As the oil industry weakened in the 1980s and funds got tight, Casbarian offered customers the opportunity to "buy a table." Table ownership included food credit, access to an exclusive stock of wines, and a private phone number for priority reservations.

Arnaud's waiters talk of a gentlemanly ghost, wearing a turn-of-the-century tuxedo, who always appears just when the restaurant is the busiest. He favors the far left corner of the main dining room near the beveled glass windows where he stands smiling at the crowded room. This specter is said to be Count Arnaud himself, making sure the waiters are satisfying customers. The Count, always strict about providing service in the grand French style, will adjust silverware and napkins if a table is not set properly. He has also been known to rearrange the bar setup and peruse the kitchen for misdeeds. His active spirit scares newly hired busboys who, startled by the sudden appearance of the old Count, drop their laden trays. When glasses shatter and knives and forks bounce off the floor, the Count is on the premises. Another ghost is often spotted drinking at the bar after closing hours. In period clothing this Creole raises his glass to toast an unseen entity; no one knows who he is or what he is celebrating.

Germaine died in 1983 and her spirit is said to haunt the restaurant as well. She is most often seen in the second-floor Mardi Gras museum, which displays a collection of more than two dozen authentic Mardi Gras costumes and carnival masks adorned with flamboyant feathers and faux jewelry. Vintage photographs, elaborate krewe invitations, and party favors give visitors a peek at the excesses enjoyed by Mardi Gras royalty. Employees and patrons report a misty form in a flowing gown hovering a few inches off the ground among the lavish gowns and royal keepsakes of Queen Germaine. Waiters complain of an eerie atmosphere in the wine cellar, where they hear raspy breathing and feel unseen hands. Psychokinetic occurrences are not unusual in the restaurant—table settings move, silverware is mixed up, and napkins are adjusted. A longtime waiter has reported seeing a woman sporting a quite large hat exiting the ladies' room and strolling across the corridor, before disappearing through the wall.

In the Richelieu Bar, one of the oldest structures dating from the late 1700s, sudden drops in temperature have been reported. According to old newspaper accounts, this property, acquired by the Count and annexed to Arnaud's, once housed opium dens and houses of prostitution. Perhaps the spirits here are not happy with the new legalities. Today Casbarian's children act as vice presidents of the family restaurant, which serves Creole dishes including frog legs and alligator sausage. The museum shrine to Germaine is free and open during restaurant hours, seven days a week. *Esquire* magazine named the French 75 Bar as one of the best cocktail bars in the country, a testament to the premium spirits, handcrafted cocktails, and fine cigars served here.

Dan had a funny feeling that something strange would happen tonight. Gloria seemed distracted from the moment they entered Arnaud's. "What's the matter?" he asked, but changed the topic after she responded twice with, "Nothing." Gloria knew the time had come to share her secret with Dan. She was worried about keeping this information from him. She still had trouble predicting his moods after all these years and was afraid he would not take the news gently.

Dan's concern allowed various scenarios to swirl in his mind. Was one of the children having marital problems, talking divorce? Or maybe their son Paul had lost his job at the bank? Who would provide for his four little ones? Then it hit him like a ton of bricks. Gloria was ill, something really serious. His heart was pounding wildly as they finished ordering and looked across the table into each other's eyes.

Gloria was glad to have the Count by her side. She began slowly. "Dan, I have been keeping a secret." Dan's heart tightened. "What is it?" he asked, alarmed that something was really wrong with his best friend and companion of fifty years. "You might not believe. . . ." Gloria looked up over her left shoulder and the words began to pour out, "You don't know it, but Count Arnaud is standing here with us. At this table. Right here. You can't see him, but I can. It's not a figment of my imagination. I can really see him, and we visit every year we come to Arnaud's. I know this is a fantastic tale, but . . ." She stopped, wondering what her husband would say. Dan gasped. "Oh, is that all? I know all about you and the Count." He smiled broadly. "You do?" Gloria said incredulously. It was Dan's turn to reveal a secret. "You know how I insist on visiting the Mardi Gras museum every year?" he started. "Yes, sort of strange, but it's our tradition," Gloria affirmed. "Well," Dan continued, "Germaine is always waiting for me there. She's such a kick. She told me how her father has a little crush on you. I wondered how long it would be before you told me . . . fifty years, eh?" Their secrets were out. Dan and Gloria reached for their wine glasses and laughed out loud . . . together.

Part Three

HAUNTED HISTORIC PLACES

New Orleans is one of the most historically significant cities in the United States. The Crescent City and
her citizens hold on to centuries-old social, festive,
and religious traditions. Family names and connections are extremely important as are where one grew
up, went to school, or attended church. Much of New
Orleans history is rooted in the French culture, integral to the city's settlement years and early customs,
but the Spanish exerted their influence as did African
slaves, islanders, Germans, Italians, and ultimately
the Americans who came for fame and fortune after
the Louisiana Purchase.

Sightseeing in New Orleans means learning about
the city's past. Preeminent historical places such as
the Ursuline Convent, the St. Louis Cathedral, and
aboveground "cities of the dead" have strange and
foreboding tales to tell. Ask your cemetery tour guide
about Marie Laveau and Josie Arlington, whose spirits
roam the graveyards frightening mere mortals. Trou-
bled spirits, such as the desolate Julie, are not only
found in the Vieux Carré, but in other sections of the

city as well, including Madame Mineurecanal in Marigny and the angry ghosts at the old Carrollton Jail site. Don't be afraid to visit the eerie old pharmacy or see a play at Le Petit deep in the French Quarter. The ancient spirits still inhabiting these old buildings are waiting for you.

Chapter 19

Vampires Go to School

The Old Ursuline Convent at 1112 Rue Chartres is one of the oldest surviving structures in New Orleans. It has survived two major fires that destroyed most of the city, numerous hurricanes, even rebellion and insurrection. The convent was built for the Ursuline nuns who did much for the disadvantaged in the city. Here young women were taught English and French, soldiers wounded in the War of 1812 were nursed back to health, and the poor and sick were comforted. The convent has a special place in the annals of New Orleans and in the hearts of its citizens. Stories abound of the good that the dedicated nuns were able to accomplish in harsh times and with limited resources. Today, looking at the graceful classical design, well-manicured gardens, iconic courtyard statues, and lovely St. Mary's Church, adjoining the convent and added in 1845, it's hard to believe the well-preserved landmark—some say by the grace of God and the patronage of Our Lady of Prompt Succor—is nearly 250 years old. Of course, there are lingering spirits here with haunting stories to tell about the sacred edifice.

Sharon and Lynda were at it again. They held vastly different views on the same subject. It had been that way most of their lives, though the sisters were born only a year apart. Sharon was a writer of historical fiction and loved delving into past lives and how fortunes were gained and lost. Lynda was a professor of history at Tulane University and depended not on lore and hearsay, but on scholarly research, to defend her theories. This afternoon, the women settled themselves in a small restaurant not far from the Old Ursuline Convent, and each tried to convince the other that her version of the tale regarding *les filles a la cassette* was not only plausible, but correct.

Sharon started off, reiterating her perspective and emphasizing in no uncertain terms that she had done enough reading to know she was right. Lynda, less boisterous than her older sister, maintained that popular opinion was not conclusive; if one scoured scholarly articles, one would know an alternative storyline must be considered. They had hoped to tour the convent but were out of luck. The doors were boarded, and a sign said the building was closed for repairs. No one was on the premises, the note advised, but for information a phone number was posted. The sisters had an hour or so before heading home for dinner, and so they sat, sipping their coffee, debating and battling the issue, both making valid points. In serious contention was why the archbishop had ordered the attic windows to be secured with eight thousand screws, blessed by the church, and sprinkled with holy water. But dusk was falling over the French Quarter, and it was time to go their separate ways, no matter that they hadn't solved the mystery. If nothing came up to thwart their weekly get-together, they would be debating another myth next Thursday.

They headed down the street toward the convent and their parked cars. Sharon looked up at the convent for a last glimpse of the graceful edifice so prominent in New Orleans history and suddenly clutched her hand over her mouth. Her other hand flew up like a flag. This gesture made Lynda look in the direction her sister was pointing. A third-floor shutter on the old convent was swung wide open, and a dim light shone from the dark interior. The two women scurried off to tell the patrolmen in the area that something was amiss in the old convent. When they reached a policeman, however, he didn't seem in the least concerned. "Oh, we get those alerts every so often," he said. "But by the time I get over there, the shutter will be closed and screwed shut tight as a drum. Don't worry, we haven't had a vampire murder in a while," he laughed. The women knew he was not going to investigate and forced a smile as they sulked away, the allusion to a vampire murder roiling in their brains. To get to their cars, they had to pass the convent again. "Thank goodness, the gate is locked," Lynda said as the women hurried by. Then mysteriously, the gate swung silently open. . . .

The first Ursuline Convent, a three-story, exposed timber French Colonial, was commissioned to house the Ursuline nuns who had arrived from France in August 1727 aboard the *Gironde,* at the request of the outgoing governor, Jean-Baptiste Le Moyne de Bienville. The arduous journey nearly saw the nuns lost at sea or to pirates or disease. Among the twelve sisters who arrived in the mud hole that was New Orleans were Mother Superior Marie Tranchepain and eighteen-year-old Sister Marie Madeleine, whose daily journal faithfully recorded the people and places of old New Orleans for present historians to peruse. The mission of the Ursulines was to care for the poor and sick and to educate young girls. Their convent at 301 Chartres was completed in 1734, and it boasted a remarkable architectural wonder, a curving cypress staircase that seemed to float on air. Less than ten years later, the building was uninhabitable. Set on unstable swampland, the walls shifted and the floors sunk in the muck. In 1745, the city's chief engineer, Ignace François Broutin, drew up plans for a new convent. Builder Claude Joseph Villars Dubreuil began construction in 1748 on a Louis XV–style edifice in half-timber (colombage) construction and lime plaster stucco-covered brick. The building, replete with arched openings, a soaring roof with dormers, and casement windows, was enhanced even further when the beautiful floating staircase from the first convent, saved from demolition, was installed in the new structure. The Ursuline Convent is the oldest building, and this staircase is one of the oldest surviving architectural pieces, in the entire Mississippi Valley.

The new convent was put to immediate use as an orphanage and a school for young girls of the area. Times were hard, as recorded by Sister Madeleine, and the populace was diverse, composed of soldiers, miners, slaves, loose women, Choctaws, and exiled criminals sent from France to populate the colony. But the territory needed growing families to be successful. That this was a priority of the king is undisputed; however, the type of woman sent over to New Orleans has been at the root of much controversy.

The first story goes that the king of France asked the Catholic diocese to send young orphan girls being schooled in convents in France to New Orleans not only to find respectable men to marry, but also to help spread Catholic teachings. Each girl carried a small, coffin-shaped trunk that contained her meager belongings. Because of its distinguishable shape, the chest was called a "casket," and the young women were called "les filles a la cassette" or "casket girls." Unfortunately, some immigrants did not survive the long journey, some girls were stolen or smuggled off the ships, and others disappeared from the convent after their arrival. The Ursulines provided a safe place for all the girls in their care, feeding, clothing, and educating them until husbands could be found.

Another legend has it that to populate the area, well-to-do, loyal French families were enticed to send their daughters to New Orleans to marry the handsome, respectable colonists of means eagerly awaiting future brides. The nuns of the Ursuline Convent welcomed the young aristocratic ingénues with open arms. As a symbol of their dedication to the wishes of the church and France, each was given a beautiful chest, called a cassette, crafted by religious artisans and intended as dowries. It is believed that twenty-eight young women, carrying Bibles, rosaries, and relics of their patron saints, arrived with their wedding trousseau in cassettes that were stored in the attic until proper suitors were found and marriages arranged. In the meantime the girls were taught languages, arithmetic, geography, history, sewing, and housekeeping.

Still a third version exists: The girls sent over to marry were of various backgrounds, not least among them women of ill repute, debtors, and workhouse rejects. The sisters were shocked to discover the background of the women and secreted them away to live in small cell-like rooms on the third floor until they were groomed and made presentable enough to meet the eligible men in the colony. Many girls felt imprisoned in the convent and frequently escaped, most often at night.

Whichever version you care to believe is up to you, but what remains is the legend that, when the marriage contracts were settled (whether with strict religious girls, aristocratic daughters, or reprobates), the cassettes were retrieved, but they were found to be empty when they were opened. And here the ghostly stories begin with tall tales of vampires and death. Some believe that vampires, having overstayed their welcome in the Old World, made their way to New Orleans in the chests accompanying the women bound for new lands. They hid in the trunks during the day and roamed the streets at nights looking for victims. Others say some of the girls themselves were vampires who fled France when their ghastly activities came under the watchful eyes of an exiled pope.

Plausible reasons for the vampire stories have been attributed to the circumstances of the newcomers' arrival. The women had survived a long, hard journey across the Atlantic Ocean with little nourishment. They were relegated below deck, with no fresh air or sunshine, and spent most of their time pining for their homeland. They disembarked the ship thin, pale, and gaunt; some were deathly ill. Doubters say the vampire tales started because some girls had contracted tuberculosis on the voyage and were so sick they were coughing up blood.

New Orleans folklore says that the original caskets of these potential brides are still in the attic of the convent and that late at night the attic shutters open and the vampires escape. They attack unsuspecting victims, then return and close the shutters before dawn. But is this more than a tall tale? The author of *New Orleans Ghosts III* reports seeing, during an unauthorized entry to part of the old convent, some small coffinlike boxes resembling the ones carried by the Casket Girls. Are they really still there? Larry Montz, an internationally recognized parapsychologist, scientist, and author, investigated the convent for paranormal activity.

When he got to the third floor, he found the atmosphere upsetting and unsettling.

Stories of vampires have flourished for 250 years in the back alleys and crime-ridden streets of New Orleans, a city plagued with a high murder rate, unexplained disappearances, and mysterious deaths. Occultists say the invisible threshold separating the living and the dead is easily crossed in New Orleans. Sometime between 1918 and 1934, Archbishop John William Shaw, the eighth archbishop of New Orleans, tried to put a stop to the vampire stories. Shaw, responding to a rise in anti-Catholicism and the growing presence of the Ku Klux Klan, is said to have ordered the heavy shutters on the eleven attic dormers to be closed and sealed. Some say it was his successor, Archbishop Joseph Francis Rummel, who demanded that each window be secured with eight thousand blessed screws and forbade anyone but high-ranking members of the church to go up there.

Today the convent is home to ecclesiastical offices and a repository for the archives of the archdiocese. Tourists are welcome to tour the museum, St. Mary's Church with its spectacular altar, the walled courtyard, and the beautiful gardens. Some say the vampires are gone, but ghosts remain. The locked gate swings open, pushed by unseen hands, and then locks itself again. Stairs are closed off to visitors, but specters of nuns are often seen ascending and descending, silently carrying out their duties. Ghost hunters have reported seeing apparitions in traditional black habits, with dark rosaries hanging from a leather waistband. Others have seen spectral figures of nuns as they move about the first floor where psychic investigators have detected the energy of many spirits, including sick

and injured children. Visitors have spotted a partial apparition of a tall man in a blue uniform in the convent garden. A story from the 1970s tells of curious ghost hunters
who saw a window shutter open and hid in the courtyard
to photograph the vampires. Their bodies, drained of all
their blood, were found the next morning. A more recent
story is told by a tour guide who said that, about two
weeks before Hurricane Katrina, he noticed that a shutter was missing on one of the windows. The next night he
noticed that the window had been bricked up from the
inside. Nine days later, after a priest had been flown in
from Rome to bless the nails, the shutter once again was
closed and secured.

Lynda hadn't seen the gate opening. Intrigued by what
the patrolman had said, she was searching "vampire murders" on her phone. "Listen to this," she read. "In 1933,
two separate Royal Street murder victims, on two different
nights, had their throats torn out. Officials on the scenes
were struck by the absence of blood. A local witness said
he saw a dark figure huddled over one of the bodies, and
when he began to scream for the police, the figure left,
walked confidently up the twelve-foot wall at the end of
the alley as if it were a level sidewalk, and disappeared."
She scrolled down and continued, "In 1984, nine people
were found in and around the French Quarter, murdered by
having their throats torn out. The police said something,
or someone, had removed all traces of blood. Rumors at
the time pointed to a rogue vampire who was destroyed by
his superiors because he had brought too much attention

to the vampire community. Both cases remain unsolved to this day." Lynda was conflicted; she had believed the aristocratic version of the Casket Girls and wasn't sure she could accept the vampire theory. "Well," said Sharon, always ready for a good story, real or fiction. "Just because they didn't hitch a ride with the Casket Girls, doesn't mean they aren't here."

Chapter 20

Père Dagobert Sings
a Phantom Requiem

The St. Louis Cathedral, Cathédrale Saint-Louis, Roi de France, is one of the most notable landmarks in New Orleans. Squarely facing Jackson Square and the Mississippi River, three symmetrical steeples reach high into the ancient Vieux Carré sky. Flanked by historic neighbors, the Cabildo and Presbytere, the St. Louis Cathedral is at the center of French Quarter life. Worshippers have attended churches on this site since 1718, when a small wooden parish structure, dedicated to Louis IX, sainted king of France, was first built for the young parish. In 1727 a larger church, using French "brick between posts" construction, was erected. Unfortunately this building along with the priest's house burned to the ground in 1788. A new, bigger church, now raised to the status of cathedral, was completed in 1794 as a gift from the wealthy Don Andres Almonester y Roxas. The cathedral expanded in 1850 to serve a growing parish and was dedicated a minor basilica in 1964, by Pope John Paul VI. Today visitors, if they listen hard enough, can sometimes hear the sad songs of those whose lives began and ended in the stately cathedral.

David had thoroughly enjoyed his high school reunion. It had been awesome to meet up with all his old buddies from his Jesuit high school, and staying the night at his friend Rick's place in the French Quarter had been an added plus. But the timing of "boys night out" could not have been worse. David had to leave the apartment just before dawn to pick up his family and make it to his daughter Lilli's 8 a.m. soccer game in Baton Rouge. Ruby had just texted him to get a move on it. David crept around the apartment, carefully trying to hush the creaking floorboards. No need to wake Rick, he thought. He gently opened the old oaken door and was unexpectedly greeted by the heavy humid air of an approaching rainstorm. He would have to hurry through Jackson Square to retrieve his car from the public parking lot behind the French Market before it started pouring. As he neared the St. Louis Cathedral, the pale purple of dawn was just creeping over the levee and a gentle mist was starting to soak through his clothes. Though there were a few late night–early morning stragglers, David thought it strange that someone should be out this early on the near-empty streets, singing. Listening closely he recognized the Latin hymn he knew so well from Mass as a child, before the English service was allowed. He began to sing along, "Kyrie eleison, Christe eleison, Kyrie eleison." When he looked toward the cathedral, he saw a well-dressed man in period clothing walking most reverently, as though leading an invisible ceremonial procession. Strange things do happen in the Quarter, he mused. David noticed a weathered old woman opening the door of a small bakery shop as if nothing out of the ordinary was happening. He was short on time but stopped to ask about the singing. "Does that man sing every morning?" he asked the petit boulangerie manager. "Oh, monsieur, you are very lucky this morning," she replied. "You are hearing the beautiful singing of Père Dagobert. Come, have some coffee and pastry with me and I will tell you a wonderful story." David knew this day was going to be special. . . .

In the 1760s, New Orleans was a thriving French colony in the New World. Its citizens, proud to be French, were prospering and enjoying all the opportunities the absentee government afforded them. The town had a Parisian air about it, fueled by the governorship of the Marquis de Vaudreuil, who modeled life in the colony after Versailles in France. Citizens sought to outdo one another in the latest fashions and social events. Commercial enterprises were developing: shipbuilding, sawmills, and other river-related industries. But this period of peace and prosperity was to come to an end. On November 23, 1762, King Louis XV of France ceded New Orleans and portions of Louisiana lying west of the Mississippi River to his cousin, King Charles III of Spain, in the Treaty of Fontainebleau. This pact was kept secret, and for a while the city was both abandoned by France and unclaimed by Spain.

The French citizens finally heard their fate when the acting governor of Louisiana, Jean Jacques-Blaise D'Abbadie, announced the news. Chaos erupted immediately. They were still in shock in March 1766, when the first Spanish governor, Don Antonio de Ulloa, arrived in New Orleans. His first order of business was replacing the French flag with the Spanish one. The people organized a local army to rebel against the detested Spanish authority, the first revolution on American soil against a European government. The rebel army overran the Spanish soldiers and ousted them from the city. As the Spaniards retreated to Havana, Cuba, the citizens thought their takeover had been successful. And it had, for a while.

It was three years before Spain sent another governor to rule the colony. When Don Alejandro O'Reilly, a Catholic Irish expatriate who had joined the Spanish army during the Spanish Inquisition, marched into town, there was no doubt which foreign power ruled the colonists. The illustrious General O'Reilly, to be known in New Orleans history books as Bloody O'Reilly, arrived with a flotilla of twenty-four ships and 2,600 soldiers. He immediately seized the Place D'Armes, the city's central area, raised the Spanish flag, and brazenly changed the square's name to the Spanish Plaza de Armas. A census conducted by the newly arrived Spanish government shows that New Orleans had only 3,200 inhabitants. The Spanish soldiers' pervasive presence was an undeniable sign that Spain meant to hold on to her new territory in America. O'Reilly dissolved the Superior Council of the French régime and installed the Cabildo, the Spanish legislative representative of Spanish authority. O'Reilly's next order of business was to find the men who had led the insurrection against Ulloa a few years earlier. This was accomplished pretty quickly; it had been no secret who had led the charge. But then the unthinkable happened. Though the citizens knew that they would be punished for their rebellious behavior if the Spanish returned, they were not prepared for the indignity imposed by a fellow Catholic. Acting as judge and jury, O'Reilly decreed the death penalty and declared that the bodies of the men would remain in the dirt in front of the Church of St. Louis to decay and rot in full view of the city. This was his way of teaching a lesson, not only to the rebels involved, but to anyone thinking about defying Spanish rule.

O'Reilly knew his actions were an affront to the people of New Orleans. Catholic burial was sacrosanct among believers, and New Orleans was a Catholic colony. That another

Catholic would so offend them, and God Himself, was unimaginable. Nevertheless, it was so ordered; Spanish soldiers would stand guard over the bodies, making sure they were not removed. The families of the fallen men appealed to their spiritual leader, Père Dagobert, for help. The Capuchin monk, Father Dagobert de Longuory, had become pastor of the Church of St. Louis in 1745. Known for his love of the people, his appreciation of bountiful food and drink, and his celebration of the good life, he was a favorite priest, often sought out for his wisdom and mercy. The families pleaded with the priest to do something to lay the souls of their dead relatives to rest.

Dagobert was outwardly outraged at the treatment of his parishioners, both dead and alive. He understood the outcry for proper burials and could not stand idly by and watch the desecration of the bodies of those who had been the most loyal of his flock. Dagobert visited O'Reilly on two occasions to beg for permission to bury the bodies, but his pleas were refused and the priest was threatened with his own imminent death if he did not desist in his entreaties. Dagobert knew he had to do something; perhaps a miracle itself was needed. One night, as dark, forbidding rain clouds swept over the city and rolling thunder cried out for reconciliation, Dagobert made his move. He visited the homes of the dead men and urged the families to secretly meet him in the priests' house, hoping the rainy, misty cover of night would shield their flight through the city. A short time after the families had assembled, Dagobert appeared and led them across the alley to the church vestibule. Before their gaping eyes lay the bodies of their dead husbands, fathers, brothers, and sons, wrapped in black cloth and placed lovingly in front of the altar.

Funeral services were performed, and the men received the last rites from their beloved pastor. The sorrowful elegy, *Kyrie eleison* (Lord have mercy), and the *Requiescant in pace* (May they rest in peace) were sung as prescribed by church liturgy—and, all the while, not a soldier was to be seen. When the requiem Mass was over, Dagobert threw open the doors of the church and beckoned family members to lift the pine coffins from the floor and follow him. The quiet, mournful procession moved slowly in the dimly lit dawn of a new day, a day that would not be marred by Catholic bodies rotting in the sun, to St. Peter's Cemetery where the blessed remains were entombed with full religious rites.

No soldier ever recounted hearing or seeing anything that night. No one could attest to what had happened. The citizens of New Orleans, if they knew anything, refused to give up the name of he who had laid the rebels to everlasting rest. Dagobert had bravely defied O'Reilly, evading the watchful eyes of the entire Spanish garrison.

The miracle of that rainy night in old New Orleans lives out today when visitors and residents turn their heads toward the saintly singing that echoes off the walls of the church and through the narrow alleys on misty mornings. As the voice grows loud enough to be heard above the rain and wind, eyes inevitably scan Jackson Square and the St. Louis Cathedral to catch a glimpse of the departed soloist. Many people have admitted hearing and seeing the phantom funeral procession led by Père Dagobert; his apparition is almost regarded as documented history.

Père Dagobert was eventually replaced by the first Spanish priest, Father Antonio de Sadilla, but he lived out a long and happy life in New Orleans. He was appointed vicar general of the diocese and was active in religious service for more than fifty years. When he died in 1776, on the eve of US independence from colonial powers, he was buried under the altar in the Church of St. Louis, what is now the St. Louis Cathedral-Basilica. Dagobert had been a champion of the people, and his haunting of the old city is endearing and cherished. The Cathedral-Basilica of St. Louis, King of France is the oldest Catholic cathedral in continual use in the United States.

David was enjoying his coffee as the old woman continued to explain the phenomenon he had just seen and heard. "Cher," said the Creole woman addressing him, "Père Dagobert only sings in the early morning rain when the city is blessed with His grace. It's praise to the miracle of life after death, don't ya think? And isn't his voice the most beautiful you've ever heard?" David looked across the square, following the specter with his eyes as the phantom procession turned the corner and disappeared. He shook his head to clear his mind and looked down at his watch. He could still make it home in time to get to the soccer game. Ruby would never believe why he would be late getting home, but perhaps this would be his lucky day and she would forgive him.

Chapter 21

Voodoo in
St. Louis Cemetery

New Orleans is a unique blend of diverse cultures often evidenced in the hard-to-pronounce names of restaurants, streets, and other places of interest. But three of the oldest cemeteries in the city are simply named St. Louis Cemetery No. 1, No. 2, and No. 3. Perhaps this lack of creativity in names reflects death as a daily occurrence in the lives of early citizens. St. Louis Cemetery No. 1 was the final resting place of departed souls as early as 1789, when the old St. Peter Cemetery was stretched beyond its limits after the devastating fire of 1788 in which 856 of the city's 1,100 structures were destroyed and many citizens perished. Frequent smallpox, cholera, and yellow fever epidemics meant room for many more graves was in constant demand. In St. Louis No. 1, aboveground vaults resembled miniature homes set on winding pathways, earning the morbid epithet, "City of the Dead." The spirits of those who have not yet "crossed over" remain behind amid the ancient gravestones to remind visitors of the interdependent nature of life and death.

Karen was in a frenzy. She had woken up late, and her mother, Louann, was anxiously rushing her out of the house. "It's not like they won't still be there when we arrive," she said, mostly to herself. She knew better than to let her mother hear her mocking their tradition of visiting the dead and decorating graves on All Saints' Day, the day after Halloween. Most of her friends went to the cemetery on All

Souls' Day, November 2, and that made more sense to her, especially if one was still exhausted from late-night Halloween parties. And her Halloween party had been a fantastic success. Now she was paying the consequences. Karen was proud of her long heritage, but she was not ready to face the "regulars" she knew would be there, like old Mrs. Monnette with her "Hello, there, dawlin'" so early in the morning. They would start with St. Louis Cemetery No. 1 and then head to the newer Metairie Cemetery.

The two women got out of the parked car, laden with plastic vases, freshly cut flowers, scouring pads, and cleaning fluids. It usually took an hour to set things right. Karen was ready to be done; she wanted to call her friends and see what they thought of last night's party. Her mother was already chastising her to hurry, and yet, she stopped at the entrance to read again the warning on the old gate: VISITORS ARE WELCOME BUT ENTER THESE PREMISES AT THEIR OWN RISK. NO SECURITY OR GUARDS ARE PROVIDED, AND THE NEW ORLEANS ARCHDIOCESAN CEMETERIES CLAIM NO RESPONSIBILITY FOR THE PERSONAL SAFETY OF VISITORS AND THEIR PROPERTY. A funny feeling crept up her neck. When a frightened cat ran across her path, she froze. "What was that?" she asked her mother, but Louann was already bustling down the narrow path toward the old family vault. The pesky feline appeared again at her heels, intent on following her. Karen tried to shake it off but couldn't. "Okay, come along then," she cajoled and then was suddenly aware why the cat was so insistent on staying close. A huge snake was lolling atop one of the larger vaults; Karen was so petrified she couldn't even scream.

By the 1780s settlers were pouring in from France, Spain, Haiti, and America looking for better lives, new opportunities, and lucrative business ventures. People died pursuing these dreams. Prominent citizens were afforded burial within the church, but ordinary citizens were not. It is not known where bodies were interred in the earliest years; most historians say graves were dug in the highest ground, the natural levees of deposited soil carried down the Mississippi River. Royal Military Engineer Adrian DePauger included a cemetery in his 1721 city plan. St. Peter Cemetery was a damp, swampy area where open ditches drained excess water from around the grave sites. Burial space in the church and St. Peter Cemetery quickly reached maximum capacity. When it was suggested that noxious interment odors contributed to outbreaks of disease and infection, the Spanish government established a new walled cemetery far outside the city limits. In 1789, land north of the French Quarter, at the corner of St. Louis and Basin Streets, became St. Louis Cemetery.

When the Americans took over in 1803, inground burial was forbidden, except, of course for pauper graves. Wagonloads of dirt were constantly hauled in to cover the remains of the indigent disintegrating in unmarked soggy, gurgling graves, and to build up the ever-sinking ground in preparation for another layer of bodies. The first aboveground tombs were "oven" vaults constructed around the outer cemetery wall, and they acted as simple, functional burial chambers. Later, plastered and whitewashed brick mausoleums topped with barreled and gabled roofs were constructed by wealthier families, civic and military associations, and benevolent organizations. These structures, housing one to four caskets, were often designed by famous architects and artists, creating an eerie labyrinth of architectural beauty. Burial places in the mausoleums were in high demand and could be rented out or sold to those needing a proper resting place for a loved one. This practice resulted in multiple, unrelated names listed on the doors of the tombs. After one year and a day, coffins could be removed and the bagged bones of the deceased either pushed to the back or dropped into a holding area below, a caveau, leaving room for another body.

Apparently a few souls refuse to leave the mazelike necropolis. The most famous ghost in the cemetery is Voodoo Priestess Marie Laveau, born to free persons of color in the French Quarter in 1801 and baptized in the St. Louis Cathedral by Père Antoine. The caramel-colored beauty dressed in simple cotton dresses and tignon and used the herbal skills she learned from her grandmother to care for those wounded in the Battle of New Orleans. Marie did not attend school and remained illiterate, signing official documents with an "X." Marie married Jacques Paris, a free quadroon émigré from Saint-Domingue who disappeared in 1823. Marie, going by the name "Widow Paris," turned to hairdressing to support herself. Calling on rich women in their homes, she overheard the latest gossip and was privy to secret confessions of love and betrayal. Openly practicing voodoo rituals gained her a reputation as a healer with divine powers. Before long she met Louis Christophe de Glapion, a handsome, aristocratic white man, who supported her until his death in 1855.

The bustling port city of New Orleans was suffering. Open sewers, rotting produce, cemetery stench, and mosquito-infested swamps allowed malaria, yellow fever, tuberculosis, and dysentry to run rampant. Marie dispensed indigenous herb potions, gris-gris charms, holy water, and incense to ease the pain of dying. She cared for prisoners and fought against the death penalty and public executions. Death was Marie's life. She buried a husband, a lover, sons and daughters, mother, and grandmother, but through these sad times, she continued to wield considerable influence over a loyal following and reigned over paganistic rituals along the banks of Bayou St. John for nearly fifty years.

Marie Laveau, Voodoo Queen, died in 1881, and her funeral procession led to the Glapion family crypt in St. Louis Cemetery No. 1, where she would receive full Catholic rites. Her apparition is not happy and warns visitors to leave. Some say she marches along the pathways chanting curses; others have felt her icy touch. She appears each St. John's Eve, June 23, to lead faithful voodoo practitioners in a wild ceremony that celebrates the summer solstice and the Feast Day of St. John the Baptist. Many have reported cold spots near her vault; others have experienced rapid breathing and headaches. A good fortune ritual is this: Turn around three times in front of Marie's tomb, knock three times to awaken her from the dead, mark the tomb with three Xs in chalk, and leave a gift. Visitors have left Mardi Gras beads, herbs, flowers, bones, voodoo dolls, bottles of rum, jewelry, and money. These offerings remain untouched; no thief dares invoke the wrath of Marie Laveau. One drifter tells of sleeping fitfully in the graveyard when he was awakened and confronted by a glowing nude woman, legs, hips, and throat entwined with a snake and surrounded by ghostly men and women dancing to drums beating primordial rhythms.

Marie Laveau is not shy and haunts people even during the day as she saunters along wearing a turban with seven knots and mumbling a loud voodoo curse to trespassers. Locals say she is alarmed by the vandalism of her tomb (as is the Glapion family who still owns the vault) and the decaying state of the cemetery. Her soul often appears as a shiny black voodoo cat with red eyes. Some say her twelve-foot snake Zombi (Zombie) is buried with her. During the day he basks in the sun atop the vault, and at night he slithers among the tombs protecting his master from those who mock her. Once Zombi followed a visitor to her hotel room, slid under the bed covers next to her sleeping body, and scared her out of her wits. The reason: She spit on Marie Laveau's grave.

Some visitors hear weeping and groaning from deep inside the crypts; others have seen Civil War ghosts and yellow fever victims restlessly roaming the maze of crypts. Taxi drivers tell spine-tingling tales of lifelike fares who disappear from the back seat once they reach their destinations. A young woman in a white dress often hails a cab near the cemetery entrance. When the cab reaches its destination, the woman asks the driver to ring the doorbell and ask for the man of the house. When the man appears at the door, apparently not for the first time, he assures the taxi driver that the phantom rider was his dead wife buried years ago in a white bridal gown. When the driver looks back to his cab, the young woman has disappeared.

Other colorful characters buried here include Delphine Lalaurie, the most hated woman in New Orleans, run out of town for extreme cruelty against her slaves, in 1842; Bernard de Marigny, a Creole plantation owner who introduced the game of craps to the United States, in 1868, and Homère Patrice Plessy, of the civil rights *Plessy v Ferguson* Supreme Court decision, in 1925. In 1884, Paul Morphy, the world chess champion and notorious recluse, was laid to rest just a stone's throw from Marie Laveau. His ashen, solitary ghost is often seen lost in thought, hunched over a phantom chess set. Another spirit is Henry Vignes, a tall sailor in a white shirt with piercing blue eyes that search interminably for his tomb. Before he left port, Henry gave papers to his burial vault, his only possession, to his landlady to keep for him. She sold the tomb while he was away at sea, hoping he would never return. But he did, and when he died, he was buried in the indigent section of the cemetery. Grave diggers say his ghost appears ragged and lost, inquiring where his vault is. Henry also walks up to guests at burials, politely touches them on the shoulder, and asks if there is room in the tomb for him, sighing "I need to rest!" before disappearing into thin air.

Alphonse, a lonely young man who takes flowers and vases from other tombs and puts them on his own, is often sighted. He takes visitors by the hand, introduces himself, and asks them to help him find his way home. He warns visitors to stay away from the Pinead tomb (no one knows the correct spelling). He always has a smile on his face, but then starts crying and disappears. Another ghost is Jimmy, a heavy-set man with blue eyes, missing teeth, and a foul stale smell who asks strangers for help putting flowers on his wife's grave. He seems very real and quite alive, until his apparition fades into mist. Fagen, a drunken ghostly resident, sings off-color songs and tells nasty jokes. He often asks people for a ride home. Many kindly phantom cats and dogs prowl near the oven tombs. Tour guides say these pets of long-ago cemetery keepers search for masters who are not even buried here.

St. Louis Cemetery No. 1 teems with paranormal activity, including electronic voice phenomena, shadowy orbs, and apparitions. Ghosts even show up in photos. Considered the most haunted cemetery in the world, it is listed in the National Register of Historic Places. Its picturesque decay has served as a backdrop for the films *Easy Rider* and *Interview with a Vampire*. Part of the original property has been sold, but nearly one hundred thousand people are entombed in the one square block that remains.

The serpent turned its head toward Karen and looked directly into her eyes, daring her to come closer. Karen knew the strange tales told about the phantoms lurking in this, the oldest cemetery in New Orleans, but until now she had been a disbeliever. She wouldn't go any closer; she knew whose tomb Zombi was protecting, and she went out of her way to avoid it. The cat was still following her, and she wondered if it was a real cat or a ghost cat. She spied her mother up ahead, and just beyond her was old Mrs. Monnette pouring water from a pitcher into a pewter vase. "Well," she said to the tabby. "Let's see if you are real or not." When she approached, Mrs. Monnette called out, "Mornin' dawlin'. Where'd ya get the cat?" Karen sighed with relief, patted the cat on the head, and ran to help her mother. *Maybe I was still spooked from Halloween,* she thought, as she looked to see if the snake was still resting atop the burial chamber. It was.

Chapter 22

Madame
Mineurecanal
Won't Leave

Faubourg Marigny is one of the oldest neighborhoods in New Orleans. Faubourg means "outside the city" and Marigny refers to Creole millionaire Bernard Xavier Philippe de Marigny de Mande-ville (1785–1868), one of the richest men in the world in 1800 when he inherited the Marigny estate at the age of fifteen. In 1806 he sub-divided his vast holdings creating a cosmopolitan French-speaking neighborhood, just across fashionable Esplanade Avenue, of quaint Victorian town houses and Creole cottages with European flair. Bernard, friend to Andrew Jackson and the Marquis de Lafayette, loved to gamble and is credited with bringing the dice game of craps to America. Many say this vice added to both his charm and his magnanimity. An obituary notice described him as "the last of the Creole aristocracy, one who knows how to dispose of a great for-tune with contemptuous indifference." By the early 1900s, when our tale begins, Marigny was in a steady decline not to be reversed until the 1990s.

Judy was done with losers and needy men. Today she was touring homes for sale and would start her new life. Bridget, the real estate agent, thought it strange that she wanted to bring her little beagle, Patrick, along, but Judy felt it was only right. She wanted Patrick's approval on their new residence. Judy parked the car on Royal Street near Franklin

Avenue. She was eager to move away from the drama of the past four years. All she had to do was find a place she liked in her price range. Quite a few properties were on the market, as many people had not returned to New Orleans after Hurricane Katrina. Judy had chosen five places to see today from properties posted online and others Bridget had e-mailed her about.

While they were waiting, Judy let Patrick out of the car and clicked the leash onto his collar. "Let's go for a little stroll around the neighborhood, shall we?" she said. Patrick eagerly led the way up Royal Street while Judy struggled to keep up. Halfway up the block, they met a nice old lady with a little dog and talked about the history of the area. Over the woman's shoulder she saw Bridget waving, so she said good-bye and hurried to meet up with the agent. "That was such a nice woman," Judy began when she caught up with Bridget. "I hope all the neighbors are as friendly." "Who was that, dear?" Bridget asked in her sing-song professional-pleaser voice. "The woman with the white terrier, didn't you see me talking to her?" Judy said. "Oh, dear," Bridget said, "we need to talk."

Tales of old New Orleans Creoles who die before their time are part of the fabric of life in the Crescent City. Nobody knows why the old woman did it, but what happened is legendary in the area known as Faubourg Marigny, an early settlement just beyond the French Quarter. The two-and-a-half-story Creole town house, built in the 1830s at 2606 Royal Street, did not give neighbors any indication that something was amiss. Yet behind its thick masonry-over-brick walls, a saddened widow was pining, not only for her husband who had been killed in the Spanish-American War of 1898, but also for her son who had left home, never to be heard from again. She was described as a quiet woman. Neighbors didn't know much about her, though they often saw her walking her little white terrier along the sidewalk. She was not unfriendly and would always nod to those she passed.

Late one night after the turn of the century, Madame Mineurecanal climbed to her attic with an old length of rope in her hand. She reached up high and threw one end of the rope over the attic beam, then stretched the rope to the banister of the attic stairwell, her jumping off point. She fashioned a noose, slipped the opening over her head, and prepared to die. But she was not alone. Her precious terrier had followed her up the stairs and was whimpering on the floor below. When she looked down and saw the little dog trembling with fear and apprehension, she paused. She couldn't leave him to fend for himself in such a cruel world. Madame Mineurecanal removed the noose from her neck and climbed down from the banister. She lifted her faithful friend and, after one last kiss, gently placed her hands around its neck and slowly began to squeeze. She cuddled the dead, limp body in her arms, climbed carefully back up on the railing, reset the noose around her neck, and jumped off. They would go to another world together.

But that was not to be. It seems neither woman nor dog got to the other side, and both remain in the house that held so much pain for Madame Mineurecanal. It was a long time before neighbors finally entered the house to look for the old woman. They found the bodies, together in death, hanging over the stairwell. Many wondered what had happened and why, and if they could have done anything to prevent it. After the suicide, tenants moved in and out of the home, and the property was difficult to sell. The owner told tales of the terrifying appearances of Madame Mineurecanal's moaning spirit. Cold spots were felt throughout the house, and the sounds of tiny dog paws scampering across the attic floor were reported.

Just after World War II, when housing in the area was hard to find and in high demand, the house was finally sold. Perhaps the low asking price should have alerted the Ruez family to "a problem," but it didn't and Mr. and Mrs. Ruez were happy to find a place to accommodate their extended family of their son and his wife; grandchildren Ramon and Teresa; Mr. Ruez's brother, Santos, and his family; and sometimes other brothers, Louis and Robert.

Years later and after many sad occurrences, grandson Ramon spoke out about the hauntings in an interview. He described the family's experiences with the angry spirit of Madame Mineurecanal, who terrorized the Ruez family from the start, even before they knew the story of her suicide.

Mrs. Ruez was the first to see Mineurecanal's ghost. She slept in a bedroom off the second-floor landing. One night she was reading in her room when she heard a baby crying. The infant's crib was just down the hall, outside the parents' bedroom. The baby continued to cry, so Mrs. Ruez got out of bed and went to the door. She saw a dark-haired woman bending over the crib, and thinking it was Rita, the baby's mother, wondered why Rita didn't pick up her crying child. Mrs. Ruez called out to the mother, then stomped her foot, yelling, "Rita." Hearing her name, Rita was roused from a deep sleep. She got out of bed and came to the doorway to ask what was going on. She saw a shocked Mrs. Ruez staring at her. When Mrs. Ruez looked back toward the crib, the mysterious woman was vanishing, head first, into the wall.

The next to see Madame Mineurecanal was Ramon's pregnant mother. Alone in the house one day, she went to the second floor to use the only phone, located by the stairway that led to the attic, to call her husband. While she was dialing the number, she heard the patter of dog paws. She looked toward the clicking and saw a little white terrier coming down the stairs from the attic. Following him was a dark-haired woman in a long white dress. Realizing the apparition was not human, she dropped the phone, grabbed the religious medal around her neck, and began praying as she ran down the stairs in fright. The woman went into premature labor soon after this terrifying event and delivered a stillborn baby.

Other family members began to report strange happenings, such as odd sounds coming from the attic and the moaning and crying of a woman in the middle of the night. Coming home late from work, Santos saw a ghostly woman descending the attic staircase. He said she walked out to the end of the landing and disappeared.

Ramon described how, as children, he and his sister, Teresa, were punished for misbehaving by having to sit near the bottom of the attic stairwell. Ramon often saw an unknown woman with dark brown hair and eyes descending the attic stairs, describing her as dark-complexioned and wearing a long white dress. She sometimes had a little white dog with her, he added. Teresa saw the ghost more than anyone else and took to calling her "Mini Canal." She could not say how she came to hear the woman's name, only that her interpretation came out "Mini Canal." One day cousin Alfrien and his parents were staying over. When Teresa spoke about Mini Canal, Alfrien thought it was an odd story and an even odder name. Making fun, Alfrien began singing "Mini Canal" over and over again. Later that night Alfrien woke the entire family up, screaming at the top of his lungs. When his parents turned on the bedroom lights, they saw a red handprint on the child's face as if he had been slapped.

An elderly neighbor eventually told the Ruez family about Madame Mineurecanal and her dog. She remembered only a few details from when she was a child, but that was frightening enough. The Ruez family attributed the unfortunate things that happened to them to the ghost lurking in their house: the stillborn baby, Uncle Louis's fatal car accident just after a ghostly encounter, and Robert's emotional problems, which started after he saw the ghost for the first time. Teresa reported rescuing her baby brother as he was hanging by one hand from outside the balcony railing. She was convinced that Mini Canal was trying to hurt the baby. To save her family, Mrs. Ruez had the house blessed, but the strange happenings continued. Eventually, too frightened to stay, the family moved away.

The house was bought by a Native American man who seemed to have his own troubles with Madame Mineurecanal. He decorated the white tiled floor of the entryway with etchings of angels and birds and was said to have performed ceremonies to banish the ghosts. After the man died in the house, his relatives performed rituals to ward off the spirits of the dead and to release his soul and any other souls held captive in the house by burning juniper and sage and singing incantations.

In the 1990s a young attorney from Santa Fe bought the house. Perhaps the pink stuccoed property appealed to his southwestern style, or maybe it was the low asking price.

It wasn't until he moved in that he began to hear the tall tales of a resident ghost and her little dog. He didn't report seeing Madame Mineurecanal, but one of his guests did have kindly encounters with the woman and reported "feeling" something in the rear corner of the back garden. It seems the old woman doesn't make trouble anymore; maybe the stress of too many people crowded under one roof had led her to threaten the Ruez family so persistently.

In 2010, a University of New Orleans professor bought the house, now in an in-demand area. Evidence of a resident ghost persists. The new owner reports a window that won't stay closed, even though she turns the latch to secure it, and footsteps overhead in the attic bathroom. She has heard a dog whining in the house during the night and says it's not her two dogs because they are both barking at the strange noise.

The Faubourg Marigny National Historic District is on the National Register of Historic Places. Residents say Madame Mineurecanal still takes her dog for a stroll along the narrow streets in the late afternoon.

"Do you believe in ghosts?" Bridget asked. Judy was feeling the hairs on her neck begin to stand up. She continued, "I believe the woman you were talking to is Madame Mineurecanal." The agent told Judy the whole story, from start to finish. "Neighbors who have seen her lately say she is no longer angry, but you'll have to decide if you still want to live in this area," she said. Judy needed time to think about this new development. She paced slowly with Patrick at her side. Suddenly she decided she would let Patrick determine if there was danger. He was really good at sensing things like that. She went directly to Madame Mineurecanal's house and took Patrick to the gates on either side. "What do you think, Patrick? Is this a good area to live in?" Judy asked. Patrick knew how much Judy depended on his natural instincts, and he would not let her down. He sniffed and sniffed, looked this way and that, and investigated under bushes and in flower beds. Judy knelt down in front of her friend and asked again, "Should we buy a house around here?" Patrick had made his decision, and he wagged his tail, side to side, as hard as he could. Judy understood what he was saying and waved Bridget over. "Let's get started. I'm buying a house today!" she said.

Chapter 23

Grieving Spirit Roams the French Quarter

One of the most enduring legends of lost love in the Crescent City took place at 732 Royal Street in a town house owned by a rich Creole aristocratic. The nearly two-hundred-year-old building has survived the highs and lows of opulent grandeur . . . and Southern decadence. Today the building has been restored as an art gallery by "Cajun artist" George Rodrigue, famous for his efforts to preserve the spirit of south Louisiana in art and his "blue dogs." Oddly enough, one of his most famous paintings, A Night Alone, *depicts a tale that took place in this very building, a story of New Orleans society and the fate of those who try to go against cultural mores.*

Nikki was a young artist studying at Tulane University in the Newcomb Art Department. She was busy painting most weekends, but tonight she would put her oils away and enjoy the French Quarter Art Crawl. The December night was windy and cold, and semester finals were looming, but Nikki was determined to indulge her artistic senses just a bit. She had gotten off to a late start, but the galleries were open until midnight and she had visited three already. Working her way up Royal Street, she got a text from a fellow art student that a group from school was meeting at the Rodrigue Gallery at midnight and did she want to get together for a drink? Nikki glanced at her cell phone to check the time; she was headed in that direction and would be there in a few minutes. "On my way," Nikki texted back, "c u 10 min."

Nikki spotted the gallery ahead and stopped to cross the street. As she stood at the curb checking for cars, the night air suddenly turned colder. Nikki pulled the light-weight jacket tightly to her chest, thinking that her mother would have made sure she had a heavy enough coat for her night on the town, but her mom, who would also have questioned what she was doing in the French Quarter at this hour, was back home in Slidell. She shook her head to stop the musings about how much she missed her mother's concern when a movement on the roof of the gallery attracted her attention. She realized, in fear, that a person was roaming around the edge of the roof. She hoped whoever was up there was being careful and stared intently as if trying to will the person to go back inside. As her eyes focused on the figure, she saw it was a young woman and the woman was naked. *She must be freezing,* Nikki thought. Then an icy mist began to fill the winter sky, and Nikki hurried across the street, into the gallery, to report the woman on the roof and her odd behavior. Nikki waved to her friends inside as she approached the glass door. When she tried to explain what she had just witnessed, her friend John's face went white. He cleared his throat. "That was Julie. . . ."

The town house at 732 Rue Royal was built in the early 1800s, a time of Southern grandeur at its best. New Orleans society, supported by the wealth of plantation crops and city commerce, operated according to its own rules. The rich and powerful were in control, not only of day-to-day business, but the city's nightlife as well. They were a privileged group and enjoyed their birthright. Customs were adopted that allowed them to maintain decorous facades while gratifying dark inner obsessions with women, gambling, wine, and good food. One such accepted practice among the wealthy men of the city was that of plaçage. This system allowed white men to carry on two distinct lives. His public life involved his wife, children, upstanding family, social etiquette, and gentlemanly behavior. His other life included late nights of drinking and carousing and his mistress, a dark-skinned beauty usually acquired at one of the Quadroon Balls, lavish affairs attended by octoroons (one-eighth black blood) and quadroons (one-quarter black blood). These young women were not prostitutes but rather genteel, cultured, and often well-schooled daughters of mixed blood (mulatto) mothers and influential men. They were free women but were not afforded the rights and privileges of white citizens. The balls were held to allow the two groups to meet. Gentlemen "protectors" supported them in fitting style for years, often lifetimes, presenting the women with a deed to a small cottage or paying rent on a Vieux Carré apartment. The two lives were not to overlap, and though it might be known that a man had a mistress and provided for her, it was never acknowledged in public. Men of the city would visit their mistresses in the evenings; plantation owners would visit on weekends or when they came into the city on business.

In the 1850s a wealthy, unmarried Creole man chose Julie, a beautiful and feisty octoroon, for his mistress at one of the popular balls. He made all the necessary financial arrangements to support the young girl, signed the proprietary contract with her mother, and "kept" Julie in a comfortable apartment on the third floor of an elegant Royal Street town house. The man went to great lengths to keep Julie happy. He thought she had everything she wanted: fine food, a French Quarter apartment, exquisite clothes, and expensive jewelry. He even said he loved her occasionally as he lavishly bestowed money and gifts on her. But Julie wanted more. She was deeply in love, so much in love that she said she could not live if she was not his wife.

The young man was aware that his wealth and standing in the city were tied to his family's fame and fortune, and he knew his elite family would never accept a mixed-blood marriage. He tried to explain this over and over again to Julie, but she was not to be dissuaded. After months of badgering, she devised a new plan and suggested they flee to France where mixed marriages were legal and where they could start a new life together. The man told Julie this was nonsense; he would not leave his family, much less the city he loved.

To halt the endless, absurd pleading for marriage, the young man presented a plan of his own. He was quite certain Julie would not carry out his scheme and felt that peace would finally reign once more in the French Quarter hide-away. He told Julie she would have to show how much she truly loved him by accepting a challenge. If she succeeded, he would marry her. He told Julie that to prove her love she must take off all her clothes, go up on the roof at midnight, and stay until dawn. It happened that he presented this deception on one of the coldest nights of the year. Sleet pelted the windows, and frigid winds prowled the narrow streets. He thought Julie would laugh and see the ridiculousness of his request. But just to be sure, he added, "If your love for me is true, it will keep you warm." The apartment was quite safe from the persistent icy knocks at the window pane. The young man hoped he had ended the arguments once and for all. He left Julie upstairs to answer the door, welcoming in some friends for the evening. The men played a little chess before the roaring fire. As midnight approached, Julie knew it was time to prove her love. Desperately she took off all her clothes and climbed the narrow mahogany stairs to the rooftop. Huddled in misery, she stood unprotected on the slippery slate, as freezing rain swirled around her naked body.

When the chess games were over, the men got down to some serious drinking and card-playing. It was near dawn when the young man said good-bye to his friends. He went straight to the bedroom, eager for the warmth of Julie's body, but was bewildered to find the bed empty and her nightclothes in a pile on the floor. He suddenly remembered his challenge. He ran up the stairs to rescue Julie from the treacherous cold. But he was too late; he shuddered as he held the lifeless, frozen body close to him. After Julie's death, the young man was inconsolable. He no longer smiled or took interest in his affairs. Her death had been so pointless, and he had, after all, loved her. He became a ghost of his former self. Within months of Julie's death, the man followed her to the grave; perhaps his heart had indeed been broken. Soon people began to talk about the young naked girl they saw on the rooftop on the darkest of December nights when sleet and bone-chilling temperatures rolled into the Crescent City. When the temperature dips and the winter rains fall, Julie eases out onto the roof and walks along the edge, her naked body leaning into the icy rain. Then as dawn approaches, her body falls to the ground and disappears.

After the Civil War, the landscape of the French Quarter changed. Wealthy citizens moved out, and commercial enterprises moved in. The town house was rented out to retail stores on the first floor and to apartment tenants above. Wilhelmina Mullen opened the Bottom of the Cup Tea Room, the first tearoom in the United States, and in the late 1920s moved to 732 Royal. A sepia tone picture hung behind the counter near the entrance documenting women in flapper dresses, delicately holding teacups, but seemingly anticipating something more. Charging money to tell someone's fortune was illegal, so the teahouse served expensive tea and gave "free" tea readings. Women sipped imported tea while they waited their turn to go behind the velvet curtain at the rear of the tearoom.

Many stories were told of Julie and her doomed love. Those who saw her on the roof would find no trace of her in the darkness when they searched the premises. Yet, she would return the next night, repeating her vigil over and over, but only on the coldest of nights and during the hours of midnight to dawn. Like many apparitions Julie's is predictable, but unlike most, which wear clothing, her beautiful fawn-colored body is naked. She roams the rooftop on December nights, but the rest of the year, she is indoors. A tearoom psychic reported an unexplained tapping of fingers on tables, the rhythmic clicking accompanied by the distinctive odor of magnolia oil perfume. Other tearoom employees verified this methodical drumming of fingers. Julie's reflection has been reported in the goldfish pond in the back courtyard, which is just under the window of Julie's former bedroom, and her yellow skirt has been spotted passing through doorways and in the rear courtyard. Others have heard Julie's unsuppressed giggling when they spot her.

Julie likes her magnolia oil perfume and has sprayed it on women as they enter the tearoom; she also is known to play with their hair. Julie played tricks on the few men who came into the tearoom, often shutting and locking the bathroom door, just as they reached for the doorknob to go in. Tenants of the upstairs apartments claim to see a ghostly chess set appear in one of the rooms before a young man sits down ready to play.

In the early 2000s the Mullen family closed the Royal Street tearoom, and since then the building has housed several businesses including a retail store and an art gallery. In 2010, the Rodrigue Gallery bought the empty buildings and property at 730 and 732 Royal. Strangely enough, Rodigue's work is now housed in Julie's building, strange because in the mid-1980s, Rodrigue painted *A Night Alone*, a famous portraiture of the legendary Julie atop the ill-fated roof. Julie's ghost can be seen in the newly renovated building as she runs down the stairs in a white gown, with her long, dark hair flowing behind her. Light on her feet, she moves more swiftly than humanly possible.

The Federal-style Creole town house has seen much through the years. Barred, arched ground-floor openings with fanlight transoms speak of a glorious past. But time has taken its toll, as well. The two wrought-iron balconies droop a little in front of louvered shutters on the windows. The tiny gabled window still peeks out from the doomed rooftop. Julie's ghost is best seen from the balconies of nearby apartments. Admirers of Julie can leave love letters for her in Père Antoine's garden, also called St. Anthony's garden, a small greenway behind the St. Louis Cathedral where sweet olives, sycamores, and magnolias guard the gated park and the memories of true love.

Nikki had not heard the tale of Julie and her rooftop hauntings. When John said it was a story of a woman who had died for love, Nikki wanted all the details. John agreed to tell her the whole story but only after they had ordered a drink at the bar down the street. Nikki had been a fool for love herself and felt an instant kinship with Julie. Nikki knew what she had seen and felt the spirit was trying to communicate with her. "It's a lesson to be learned," Nikki said when she heard what had happened to Julie and her young Creole gentleman. *Some things in this world never change,* she thought, looking down at her naked ring finger.

Chapter 24

La Pharmacie
Française
Concoctions

The nineteenth-century healing powers of medicines and medical treatments were often misunderstood and unproven. Physicians and apothecaries concocted strange potions that sometimes worked to rid a patient of some ill-fated disease. Other times the medicine failed, leaving death in its wake. Some medical practitioners worked diligently to help those who sought their knowledge; others engaged in wild experimentation, not caring that their conduct discredited the medical profession. In New Orleans the best and the worst coexisted. One man makes his mark on history as the first licensed pharmacist in the country; the other leaves behind bizarre tales of human experimentation. One makes his mark on the pages of history; the other is sentenced to roam the medical offices of La Pharmacie Française forever.

Kay was eager to depart for her interview at Xavier University in New Orleans. She was seeking a professorship in its College of Pharmacy. It was February and the weather in Minnesota was just awful; another snowstorm was slated for later in the week, but she was, gratefully, on the plane and would be gone long before the bad weather rolled in. Looking forward to relaxing in the beautiful French Quarter hotel the school had chosen for her brief stay, Kay had researched places she wanted to see in the city. At the top of her list was the shop of the first licensed US pharmacist. She was looking forward to discovering other pharmaceutical connections in the fabled "City That Care Forgot."

Finally able to sit back and breathe after a hectic week of preparation and packing, Kay thumbed through her interview itinerary and circled Wednesday afternoon as a good time to slip away to see the pharmacy and other places of interest. Her meetings with college administrators would be over, and she would have a few hours before the scheduled dinner with the chair of the college. Kay fully intended to fuel her passion for the vibrant and growing field of pharmacology by exploring the profession's roots firmly embedded in New Orleans's past.

The city was magical. Kay loved staying at the Hotel Maison de Ville on Toulouse Street in the French Quarter. She knew this would be an especially memorable trip when she learned her hotel had once been the home of Antoine A. Peychaud, the famed apothecary who had fled Saint-Domingue during the bloody slave revolt of 1791. In his pharmacy Peychaud had concocted the first cocktail by mixing cognac and bitters in an egg-shaped container called a coquetier. The Americans, of course, would have trouble with the French accent and pronounced the popular drink first as "coctay" and then as "cocktail." This was surely a good sign for what the next few days would hold. If she had time, she also wanted to see the old François Grandchamps' Pharmacie. This Creole apothecary was said to dispense snakeroot combined with whiskey to treat fevers, cockroach tea as a cure for tetanus, and other bizarre remedies for yellow fever, the scourge most feared by city residents. His pharmacy, still standing today, occupied the corner of Royal and St. Louis Streets and was famous for its curved entranceway that made entering from either cross street easy for patrons.

As Wednesday's interviews finally came to an end, Kay headed back to the hotel. She was tired, but she had no intention of napping on her last day in New Orleans. She quickly changed out of her professional clothes, grabbed her camera, and headed out the door to La Pharmacie Française, the apothecary that Louis J. Dufilho Jr. (sometimes spelled Duffalo), the first licensed pharmacist in the United States, opened in 1823. She was not at all concerned that the place was said to be haunted. She didn't believe in those notions anyway.

Louis J. Dufilho Jr. was born in France and studied at the Sorbonne in Paris. He immigrated to New Orleans in 1803. Dufilho, a serious man of medicine, was determined to take and pass the pharmacy exam that had been put into place by Louisiana Governor William Claiborne in answer to concerns over the lack of professional standards. Claiborne had established a committee of physicians and pharmacists in good standing to conduct oral exams for potential pharmacists. Though some informal regulations were on the books, there was no regulatory oversight by any official agency. Anyone could open a shop after apprenticing with another unlicensed pharmacist for six months. Dufilho did indeed take the three-hour Louisiana license exam given at the Cabildo, the government building where the signing of the Louisiana Purchase had ceded a vast territory from France to the United States. The building sat auspiciously on Jackson Square, newly named for Andrew Jackson, hero of the

Battle of New Orleans in 1815, though many continued to call the square the Place d'Armes. Even though the law was in place, it took twelve years before anyone passed the exam to become licensed. On May 11, 1816, Dufilho became the first licensed pharmacist in the United States.

After practicing for a few years with his elder brother on Toulouse Street, Dufilho bought the lots at 514–516 Chartres Street, where he intended to construct his apothecary, on June 5, 1822, from Philip Sadler. Dufilho opened his apothecary for business in 1823 and became quite successful. By 1837 he had hired renowned local architect J. N. B. de Pouilly to renovate his small building into a three-story porte cochere structure with an entresol level, a storage area between floors, which stands today. Dufilho's Creole entresol building of plastered brick served as his pharmacy, office, and home. Arched doors and windows faced onto the street, and fanlight windows above the openings lighted the entresol level. Dufilho could stand on the narrow gallery with wrought-iron railings on the second floor and look out over the French Quarter. His third-floor rooms were lavishly graced with individual balconies. His prosperity was evidenced by the twenty-three slaves he owned, some of whom helped with the herb and plant gardens that flourished in the slated courtyard out back.

Dufilho operated his pharmacy until 1855 when, after more than thirty years of practice, he moved back to France. Perhaps he had been worked to near death during the 1853 yellow fever outbreak, the worst in any US city, which claimed one in ten New Orleans residents. He died abroad the next year, and his apothecary and town house were then occupied by Dr. James Dupas, a pharmacist and physician. At this point the bright future for the pharmacy profession darkened despondently. Mysterious things began to happen; people were seen to enter the building but never leave.

Dr. Dupas was engaged in experimental pharmacology. The beautifully carved rosewood cabinets hid his secrets. Narcotics, herbal tonics, magical Oriental oils, lithium, cocaine, and heroin were used to cure the ill and ailing. Surgical tools were kept busy. Dupas found new and torturous ways to use scissors-like urethral dilators, blood-letting knives, primitive drills for boring into skulls, and eye scalpels. Bloodthirsty leeches sat in apothecary bottles ready to be sated.

Dupas used his office on the second floor of the apothecary shop to carry out his "work." Here he conducted vile experiments on slaves and those suffering from horrific diseases. His healing concoctions were made from poisons and ingredients used in the practice of voodoo. Treatments given to pregnant women resulted in the deaths of mother and baby or, frighteningly, in the disturbed births of deformed and disfigured babies. When death finally claimed a victim, Dupas disposed of the body through a second-floor trap door in the entresol level that dumped the remains onto a waiting wagon in the carriageway below.

Dupas carried on bizarre experiments until his death in 1867. He is said to have gone mad from syphilis. He got away with murder, it is true, but life after death sometimes has a way of evening the score. The spirit that is said to haunt the pharmacy building, which has been turned into a museum of apothecary, dental, and other medical artifacts, is Dupas himself. Museum staff members say they have seen a short, solidly built man wearing a white lab coat over a brown suit roaming through the building. The spirit appears to be in his sixties and has a mustache. His ghost has been sighted often on the stairway to the second floor, where both staff and visitors report that he gently pushes them from behind as they climb the stairs. Employees report that his spirit hovers around the shop, looking in cabinets and checking medicine bottles. His spirit can throw books, and he delights in setting off the alarm system. Dupas can even move around items in the locked display cases.

Ghost hunters from the International Society for Paranormal Research have examined the New Orleans Pharmacy Museum. They report extreme negative energy in the building. Pregnant women who venture to the second floor, which houses the large bed and medical instruments used in childbirth procedures, report shortness of breath and stabs of abdominal pain.

In the years following Dupas's death, the building had many owners; none held onto the property for very long. In 1915 a devastating hurricane ravaged the area, and the once vibrant pharmacy stood vacant and neglected for more than twenty years. In 1937 Mayor Robert Maestri bought the building and donated it to the city. Though having no formal schooling beyond the third grade, Maestri was committed to preserving the city's past as an educational opportunity for future generations. When historians pointed out the importance of the site, Maestri established the Historical Pharmacy Commission of the City of New Orleans, which initiated plans to turn the building into a museum. After extensive repairs the museum was officially dedicated on October 16, 1950, and was operated by the city commission until 1987 when it was sold to the nonprofit preservation group Friends of the Historical Pharmacy.

Today the New Orleans Pharmacy Museum displays the largest pharmaceutical collection in the United States.

Before Hurricane Katrina devastated tourism in the city, the museum attracted nearly thirty thousand visitors a year. The museum houses other medical and dental artifacts of the time period in beautiful hand-carved mahogany and glass cabinets. Numerous mortars and pestles, the centuries-old emblem of pharmacy, are on display.

The museum has two floors of exhibits. The squeaky wooden first floor is a replica of an operating apothecary, including a soda fountain (not in operation) from 1855. Here visitors can see displays of bloodletting equipment, microscopes, and cosmetics from the nineteenth century in rosewood cabinets. At the prescription counter one can learn how the pharmacist prepared and filled vintage bottles with voodoo potions, herbs, and opium and cocaine drugs used during the period. The second floor displays an examination room with a hospital bed and surgical instruments, including archaic child-birthing devices, and a library.

A courtyard hidden from the narrow street has benches for viewing the herbs and flowers used in the pharmacy trade years ago. Visitors can see aloe, used for burns; jasmine, which settled the stomach; foxglove, employed as a powerful heart stimulant; and angel's trumpet, which relieved the symptoms of asthma. Culinary herbs abound: chives, tarragon, spearmint, parsley, sweet marjoram, and more. Another spirit strolls about here in the gardens. Ghost hunters have reported a female specter that stands by the fountain near the medicinal herb garden. Perhaps she seeks to protect the expectant mothers from the phantom grip of Dr. Dupas.

Kay found the shop on Chartres Street quickly. She put her face up close to the front window, where the show globes were on exhibit. Pharmacists would fill the clear globes, fancy or plain, multitiered or simple, with colored water to entice patrons into their shops. The globes were functional, too. During plagues or epidemics, the water in the globes would be red to warn citizens of the danger of sickness lurking in their city.

Excited to finally have the chance to visit the apothecary, Kay looked eagerly through the front window. There was so much to see. She was intrigued by the wooden blenders used to mix the potions and the recipe books of healing compounds. She couldn't wait to get upstairs where the nineteenth-century sick room displayed antique wheelchairs, primitive crutches and inhalers, and spectacles and other visual aids from the period. Kay entered the pharmacy and walked straight to the stairway, but suddenly she felt an afternoon tiredness set in. Perhaps fatigue was getting the best of her after all. She decided not to make the climb. But as she began to take her foot off the first step, she suddenly felt light as air, as if someone were lifting her from behind. Her foot reached for the second step, then the third. Someone or something was gently pushing her up the stairs. She virtually glided to the second floor. That was an easy climb, she thought, as she approached the antique hospital bed and surgical instruments. Suddenly a wave of nausea swept over her, and she doubled over with pain. She turned quickly and rushed down the stairs. Perhaps something she had eaten for lunch had not agreed with her.

Kay leaned against the door frame, holding her stomach and breathing in the fresh warm air. She was still drawing in a long, deep breath when one of the museum staff walked over to her. "So, when is your baby due?" she asked. Kay's eyes shot open. "How do you know I'm pregnant?" she asked. "I haven't told anyone yet." "Oh, honey," the staff member said. "All pregnant women feel ill when they get to the second floor. I saw you fly down the stairs. I bet you felt a sharp pain in your gut, too. It's Dupas; he has that effect. Even those psychic investigators said pregnant women feel ill when they come under his spell."

Chapter 25

Rattling Chains of the Old Carrollton Jail

The area hugged by the sharp bend in the Mississippi River, where Carrollton Avenue meets St. Charles Avenue, is much beloved by residents and tourists. Chic retail stores, the famous Magnolia Café, rattling streetcars, and cozy, antique bookstores offer unique experiences for those roaming the streets of uptown New Orleans. But in the quaint establishments of a thriving business district lurk ghosts of the past. Carrollton was the area settled by the Americans, not the wealthiest merchants who established the Garden District, but those who set their roots farther upriver. The young town grew rapidly and was annexed in 1874 by the City of New Orleans, but that was later, after the tales of suffering and misery by the lawless and not so lawless incarcerated in the Carrollton Jail had become part of the local folklore.

Lauren and Emily were excited about their weekend in New Orleans, the city where their mother had been born into a ten-generation New Orleanian family. "Our ancestor, Jean Baptiste Perret, arrived in New Orleans from Grenoble, France, in 1723," Mom had told the sisters, "just five years after Jean Baptiste LeMoyne, Seur de Bienville founded the City of Nouvelle Orleans." The girls had heard the stories over and over again, but living far away in another state, they had spent little time in New Orleans. Now they were here and ready to do some exploring. First on the agenda their mother had put together for them was riding the streetcar up St. Charles Avenue. The aunt they were staying with dropped them off at the bottom of Carrollton Avenue. They waved good-bye to Aunt Elaine and headed to the streetcar stop, but the girls knew there were sights to see in this area; they had done their own research on the Internet. They were excited to find some favorite locations used by filmmakers. *The Curious Case of Benjamin Button* and *Fight Club* had been filmed in this area, not to mention *Alien* and *Larry the Cable Guy*. The girls headed for Oak Street. They crossed Carrollton and walked briskly past a large white building. But they heard something odd and stopped in their tracks. They suddenly felt a chill in the air, and the gloom of awful suffering settled over them. They tried to move their feet, but they seemed planted in the pavement. Lauren took out the guidebook their mother had given them and rifled through the pages to read about the area. There was no mistaking their location; they were in front of the Carrollton Jail, a building that had seen much suffering and death. Numerous stories of ghostly inmates returning to the grisly scene, told by hardened law enforcement officers, attested to the reality of the ancient tales. The girls grabbed each other's hands, hoping to get away before they saw or heard . . .

Carrollton grew out of land that was originally the plantation of Chauvin de la Freniere, one of the leaders of the colonial revolution against Spanish authority. La Freniere was ultimately shot in 1769 by General Alejandro O'Reilly, the second Spanish governor of the Louisiana colony who is still remembered in New Orleans as "Bloody O'Reilly." This tough Spaniard had many prominent rebel Frenchmen exiled from the territory, imprisoned for life, or executed. After la Freniere's death the property had several owners, but in 1795, the Spanish authorities awarded it as a land grant to Jean Baptiste Macarty. The land, nestled in a bend of the Mississippi River, was about five miles outside the city limits and part of the rural countryside. Of course, if you were traveling by boat, the journey up the winding river would be nearly nine miles. Macarty established his sugar plantation here to take advantage of the thriving New Orleans market and Mississippi River transportation system. In 1814, with the War of 1812 underway and the city readying itself for the Battle of New Orleans, General William Carroll settled his Kentucky militia on the river batture in this area. The unit would soon join General Andrew Jackson's army to defeat the British. It is said that General Carroll gave the area that was home to his soldiers its name, Carrollton. Much of this area does not exist today, as the riverbank there caved in and the land was lost. An upper portion of the land survived and passed into the hands of Ludgere Fortier.

The Carrollton area was growing from rural to urban, and a town was in the making. Developers had anticipated the growth spurt, and land speculators Laurent Millaudon, Samuel Kohn, John Slidell, and the Canal Bank purchased a large tract of the Macarty plantation and commissioned Charles Zimpel, a German surveyor and civil engineer, to design a street plan. Zimpel's layout was completed in 1833. The first home was built by Samuel Short (Short Street is named after him). A real estate boom ensued, and homes sprang up throughout the area, bolstered by the completion of a local steam rail line connecting Carrollton to New Orleans in 1835. Historians say this was one of the first railroads in the country. Hotels followed homes and businesses. The Carrollton Gardens Hotel, opening as a resort for city-dwellers in 1836, lured city folk to the relaxing and picturesque town. Writer William Thackeray is said to have rested here.

Carrollton was incorporated in 1845 with John Hampson, holder of a patent on venetian blind slat positioning, as mayor. Building roads to connect the city to New Orleans became important, and St. Charles Avenue was opened in 1846 and was later paved with shells. The city of Carrollton became the seat of government for Jefferson Parish in 1852, and an impressive city hall and courthouse of neoclassical architectural design was erected on Carrollton Avenue. The *Carrollton Times* reported on the growing commercial district, with furniture, clothing, and shoe stores, restaurants, fruit stands, bakeries, a lumberyard, and especially, coffee and ale houses.

As the town grew into a city, it experienced urban woes: theft, assault, bribery, and murder. It needed a jail. Originally called the Jefferson Parish Prison, the building was part of the city's administration complex and became the Ninth Precinct Station. For locals, however, it was simply known as the Carrollton Jail—a place of dread that stood for nearly a century. The two-story brick structure, with narrow stone-walled cells, had securely barred windows behind which many atrocities occurred. Hidden from public view, prisoners, riddled with disease and infirmities, often went without proper medical care. Suicides were frequent and violence was common. Convicts were hanged from gallows in the central courtyard, where the lynching of a man suspected of butchering a local child was documented.

Though the jail no longer exists, the courthouse still stands and has served the public interest as various city schools, perhaps making up for the untold lives wasted and lost in the judicial process in earlier years. Public executions were outlawed in 1854, but that didn't ensure humane conditions in the scary-looking building that housed Carrollton's criminal element.

One story, related by several eyewitnesses, tells of a man accused of his wife's murder. But this was not your ordinary murder. The husband had boiled his wife's body in lye to eradicate any evidence of his crime and then made soap of the body remains. This gruesome case did not go to trial because outraged and horrified policemen beat the man to death in jail. As the mangled man lay against the jailhouse wall, he vowed, in his last breath, to return and seek vengeance upon those who had killed him. The police officers felt justice had been served, and the man's dying words were not taken seriously until 1899, when a woman waiting in the station house to talk with Sergeant William Clifton leaned against the wall where the man had died and was suddenly thrown away and back from the wall by an invisible force. The woman was scared, but curious. She went to the wall, leaned her weight against it, and again was violently tossed off. In a panic, she screamed that something evil was in the wall and explained what had happened to the men in the room. They, too, tried to lean against the wall. All were propelled away with no apparent explanation. Sergeant Clifton was a respected officer of the law and praised highly for his command. When he told the story of what had happened in his presence, it was believed.

The wall continued to be possessed by some unknown supernatural power, and other mysterious occurrences began to happen. A few nights later, the driver of a police wagon, resting on a couch near the mysterious wall, was suddenly thrown, couch and all, across the room. This violent act was repeated the next night when another officer, doubter that he was, sought to rest on the same couch. He, too, was thrown across the room. This should have been sufficient evidence to label the wall "haunted," but the ghost was not sated in his revenge. A large portrait of Civil War hero General P. G. T. Beauregard, hanging on the demoniac wall, fell for no apparent reason and broke into pieces. The cord holding the picture remained intact and fastened tightly to the nail still embedded in the wall. A picture of Admiral George Dewey would spin unrelentingly like a wheel on its nail for no apparent reason. People began to avoid the wall.

But they couldn't avoid all the ghosts of the old jailhouse. Policemen reported hearing footsteps in the halls but upon investigation, found no one there. Paperweights flew off desks, flung ferociously at officers. One ghost tried to strangle a policeman in a courtroom remodeled from rooms that had previously been jail cells for condemned prisoners.

Prisoners were not immune to the paranormal violence. They often claimed beatings in their cells by unseen forces, especially those prisoners in cell number three. In the morning each near-death prisoner reported that three spirits had materialized through the wall and fought manically with each other during the night, whipping the real-life criminal in their raging battle. Older police officers recounted the tale of three criminals locked up in this jail cell together. In the morning, after a horrendous night of attack, all three lay dying.

Witnesses of the strange happenings were plentiful, and many stories were told by hardcore, unbelieving law enforcement officers. The spirits of two quadroon women who were convicted of cutting out the liver of their mutual lover often visited the premises, only to disappear as quickly as they had come. The varied and frequent testimonies to the array of eerie happenings in the Carrollton Jail make it seem quite possible that these events did occur, and urgent requests by policemen to be transferred to other precincts were common. By 1899 these ghostly occurrences had made their way into the local papers, documented into perpetuity.

The Carrollton Jail was torn down in 1937, but workmen at the demolition claimed to have seen ghostly figures laughing as the building fell in clouds of dust from the century-old stone. Others reported seeing human shapes writhing in the dust as the gallows were dismantled. Perhaps those executed here were returning for one last glimpse of their hell on earth, reveling in its destruction.

Emily and Lauren found strength from each other's tightening grasp to continue walking past the Old Carrollton City Hall and the area where the jail had impacted so many lives. Oak Street was just ahead, and they couldn't wait to get back to the twenty-first century. Though many historical buildings and much Victorian architecture remain, the area is alive, bright, and cheery with restaurants, coffeehouses, vintage clothing stores, and local boutiques. The women admired the proliferation of flowers and plants as the streetcar rumbling down St. Charles Avenue called to them to get aboard. And they would, but first they would lunch at La Madeleine and then search out the house where Pulitzer Prize winner John Kennedy Toole, author of *A Confederacy of Dunces,* had lived, two of their mother's favorite New Orleans spots. This was to be a nostalgic trip to be remembered.

Chapter 26

Josie Arlington's Flaming Tomb

Just after the city was founded and serious settlement began, New Orleans earned a shady reputation that has been hard to shake. To address the shortage of women in the colony, the French government released prostitutes from prison on the condition they set sail for New Orleans. Many became respectable wives, but others turned to more lucrative endeavors. A bawdy prostitution trade took root and flourished. By 1744, a French army officer affronted by the number of bordellos in the city said he would not be able to find "ten women of blameless character in New Orleans." Prostitution was rampant citywide; New Orleans was known for its harlotry. One of the more colorful figures in what is called "the oldest profession on earth" was Miss Josie Arlington, the wealthiest madam of one of the most lavish bordellos in the city, who was laid to rest in a flaming tomb in the exclusive Metairie Cemetery.

Daphne had been up all night worrying and was now headed toward Metairie Cemetery to oversee the moving of her mother's remains. A month ago, Uncle Kenneth, the family patriarch, had asked her to consider a request: "Can we have your permission to move Melda from the main part of the tomb to the bottom storage area to make room for Aunt Constance who, doctors say, will be dying very soon?" After hemming and hawing a little, Daphne said, "I'll call you back." Unsettling emotions were rising up from deep within her. When her mother died suddenly a few years ago, she had been thrust into a whirlwind of legal concerns and burial arrangements while keeping her own life on track. She loved her mother very much and still missed her terribly. Now it appeared she had a second chance to say good-bye, time to tell her all she had been thinking and feeling. A date was set for Mary Albert, the cemetery administrator, to walk her and Uncle Kenneth through the transfer process. The tomb held four caskets. Grandma and Grandpa were assured their coffins would remain in the aboveground portion. That left two spaces. A cousin had taken one spot just last year and could not be moved yet by law. Daphne understood the necessity of making room for Aunt Constance but wondered if she could consent to a process that would remove her mother's decaying bones from her coffin, wrap them in a protective covering, and lower the parcel into the dark, damp bottom area of the burial chamber, the caveau.

She did consent but called her son, Derek, to come with her to the cemetery. It was a dreary day, and thunderstorms were threatening. As they entered Metairie Cemetery, Daphne and her son walked straight to the family tomb; she knew which paths to take and where to turn. She had been here many times to adorn the grave site with pink camellias, her mother's favorite flower, and plastic Mardi Gras beads. She always walked passed Josie Arlington's tomb, giving a wave to the determined young maiden on the steps. Then she stopped, dead in her tracks. "Did you see that statue move?" Daphne asked Derek.

Miss Josie Arlington was born Mary (Mamie) Deubler around 1864, in Carrollton, just beyond the New Orleans city limits. Her German parents were strict, and "Little Mary" rebelled. When she was just seventeen years old, Mary took up with a shady gambler, Philip Lobrano, known as "Schwartz." It is said that one night when Mary returned home after curfew, her angry parents locked the door. Making her sleep on the porch would teach her a lesson. The young girl kicked and pounded on the door, waking the neighborhood. Then, in anger, she announced she was leaving and would never return. She moved in with Schwartz and worked for him in a number of low-class brothels under the name Josie Alton. Soon, as Josie Lobrano, she opened a place of her own at 172 Customhouse Street (now Iberville). She broke up with Schwartz in 1890, decided to appeal to a wealthier clientele, and rechristened her establishment Chateau Lobrano d'Arlington, taking the name from Tom Anderson's famous pre-Prohibition saloon.

In 1896, Josie moved her "Chateau" to 225 Basin Street, just a few blocks from the French Quarter. It became simply "the Arlington," a refined establishment for gentlemen willing to pay for the services of her exquisite girls. Her brothel was quite successful, but the city of New Orleans was about to make Josie even richer.

As the century neared its end, gangs, the mafia, gambling, and prostitution spread unchecked through the growing and crowded urban area. In 1897, city authorities, led by Alderman Sidney Story, embarked upon a bold experiment. To fight prostitution and gambling, they would confine these vices to one supervised area. Ironically, "The District" became known as "Storyville" after the alderman, much to his dismay. Establishments in the area ran the gamut from mansion to fleabag dump, employing more than two thousand women and many more caterers, waitresses and waiters, maids, and musicians. Some places boasted plush velvet sofas, erotic shows, mirrored walls and ceilings, and ballrooms for dancing. Musicians flocked to Storyville, playing horns, fiddles, and harmonicas until dawn. The descriptor "jazz" was used for the first time by the "Razzy, Dazzy, Jazzy Band," and soon-to-be jazz superstars Buddy Bolden, Jelly Roll Morton, and Louis Armstrong performed here. Visitors to the city frequented the bordellos and the clubs to listen to jazz and took this new sound back home with them. *The Mascot*, a five-cent weekly, devoted considerable space to the activities of the red-light district, and *The Sunday Sun* became a well-read scandal sheet.

As it turned out, Josie's four-story posh, gaudy bordello, replete with original oil paintings, lavish statuary, potted plants, lace curtains, Oriental carpets, cut-glass chandeliers, and stunning quadroon and octoroon women, happened to be located within the prescribed area. She became the reigning queen of Storyville, the most famous red-light district in the country. Josie's establishment was listed in the Blue Book directory, which described her place thusly: "Within the walls of the Arlington will be found the work of great artists from Europe and America. Many articles from the Louisiana Purchase Exposition will also be seen." Josie served the elite of the city, but she was never accepted into their social circle. The landowners, politicians, lawyers, bankers, doctors, and judges who visited her house of vice and promised enduring friendship shunned her publicly on the streets. Josie was powerful, and she vowed revenge on the society snobs who rejected her. Money was no object as Josie was financially set. She lived in a fancy house in the affluent Esplanade area, but was obsessed by the one thing she longed for—acceptance by society. Denied this respectability, she was determined to exact her revenge. She planned for her burial in the city's most fashionable cemetery. Metairie (French for a type of farm) Cemetery, originally a racetrack, had been turned into a graveyard in 1873 by Charles T. Howard, president of the New Orleans Racing Association and the Louisiana State Lottery. The circle of the track became the main drive of the park-like cemetery, which featured landscaped plots and ponds. Confederate war heroes Generals Beauregard and Jefferson Davis (later moved) were buried here. The impressive cemetery is a majestic maze of giant mausoleums and monuments where the most powerful and well-known names in the city are artistically chiseled in stone. Josie purchased a burial plot and commissioned Albert Weiblen, one of the city's most prestigious designers of funeral architecture, to build an ornate mausoleum on a raised mound overlooking the lower graves of society's high and mighty. Weiblen worked with polished red marble from Stonington, Maine, installed copper double doors with brass knockers, and topped the tomb with two blazing urns. Josie also engaged F. Bagdon to create a statue of a maiden ascending the steps leading to the vault. The maiden holds a bouquet of roses in the crook of one arm and knocks on the brass doors with the other. Josie's final legacy was a work of art . . . and very expensive.

The women of New Orleans demanded that Josie be refused burial in the upscale cemetery—her money and charm meant nothing to them—but she could not be stopped. The Storyville madam had her revenge. Soon after the tomb and statue were completed in 1911, odd things began to happen. The tomb was said to burst into erotic flames that danced along the smooth, silky surface of the marble. People came in droves to see the burning tomb and flaming urns that resembled the gates of hell. Those who lived in the area said the maiden on the steps could get very angry; her pounding on the copper doors could be heard for blocks. Some say the maiden depicts Josie herself, locked out of her house, banging the door to be let in. Others say it symbolizes Josie as an outsider in society who, no matter how hard she knocks, will never be admitted.

Josie died on Valentine's Day in 1914, at the age of fifty. From that day, reports that the statue could move began to surface. Cemetery sextons Todkins and Anthony saw the maiden leave her step to roam through the cemetery. They reported following the statue through the shelled walkways around the other graves before she simply vanished. At least twice the cemetery staff found the statue in other parts of the cemetery in the morning.

Josie's resting place came to be known as the "Flaming Tomb" because many people said they had seen the crypt burst into flames right in front of them. Many attributed the apparition of tongues of flame moving along the cold, red stone to the reflections of a nearby streetlight that swayed in the wind. The light fixture was removed, but reports of the flaming tomb persisted. Vandals moved the statue, some say, but the stone maiden is heavy and awkward, and was never damaged. Mysteriously the "Flaming Tomb" is no longer the resting place of Josie Arlington . . . or is it? Some say that, because the families of those buried in the surrounding graves feared that curiosity seekers would trample on their loved ones, the cemetery agreed to remove Josie's remains to a receiving vault in an unknown location. Another story says that Arlington left her estate to a beloved niece and her business partner, who conspired to spend all her money, dispose of her mansion, and sell her infamous burial chamber for a vast sum. Years later, the tomb was bought by J. A. Morales. Strangely enough the new owner had the same initials: "J. A." and these are etched into the top marble frieze. The tomb is still called Josie Arlington's, and neighbors continue to complain that the pounding on the doors keeps them awake on moonless nights.

Derek was afraid his mother was under too much stress. But now was not the time to alarm her, he thought. He tried to placate his mother by beginning an explanation about how atmospheric conditions on dark and rainy days can distort one's perceptions of reality. But Daphne wasn't buying it, despite her son's degree in meteorology. "No, really," Daphne said, "the statue moved. I saw it." She hesitated to say that the statue had also waved at her. Derek grabbed his mother's hand and pulled her toward him. "Let's go," he said. "Uncle Kenneth is waiting for us." Everything was in order when they got to the family tomb, and Ms. Albert was ready to begin. Daphne took a deep breath as the mausoleum door was opened and Melda's coffin extracted. She drifted away to the day of the funeral when, crying, she had bade a final farewell to her mother. The eerie sounds of the casket being opened were making her queasy and light-headed. She felt faint. Then suddenly caressing arms were around her waist, supporting her weight. She looked around at Derek and Uncle Kenneth; neither seemed to notice the maiden with the bouquet of roses, holding her up. But she knew it was her friend who had come to her rescue, the one she always waved to, the young woman perpetually climbing the steps outside Josie Arlington's tomb.

Chapter 27
Ghostly Performances at Le Petit Théâtre

Le Petit Théâtre is a major arts and performance venue in the French Quarter that many New Orleanians hold dear to their hearts. Le Petit, as natives call the theater, offers guests an array of experiences from intimate performances to lavish Broadway productions to literary festivals. With such a long history, the theater has seen elation and sorrow, success and . . . death. It is said that patrons and performers alike have stayed on beyond this world to walk the ivied balconies above the inner courtyard or sit in rapture in the audience to applaud one more outstanding performance. Many apparitions have been seen and heard in the old buildings that make up Le Petit. Perhaps the creative souls that once lived and breathed the stage have found ways to stay around the theater. The young actress, Caroline, and her tale of passion and death and Señor Venegas's unrequited love story are among the favorite ghostly tales of local patrons.

Gina and her cousin Pam were meeting at Le Petit for the Tennessee Williams Festival. They had made these plans every spring for nine years and were eagerly looking forward to this year's lectures, workshops, and performances. Celebrities were always in town for the occasion, and nightly original performances highlighted the busy schedule. Gina loved to get to town early and roam the French Quarter a little before heading over to the St. Peter Street theater.

Café au lait and beignets, a visit to the St. Louis Cathedral, and a stroll through Jackson Square got her in the "old New Orleans" mood. She always planned to be one of the first to arrive at the theater, so she could slip backstage and get a look at some of the sets that would be used for this year's performances. Gina had been a dancer when she was younger and still felt a part of the art world. She would never tire of seeing ordinary props transform into fantastical illusions as the curtain went up. The young woman quickly scanned the area for volunteers who were usually posted to keep festival guests in the entry lobby. Seeing no one around so early, she climbed the stairs to the tiled balcony. From here she could look out over the wrought-iron railing to the courtyard fountain below and imagine the comings and goings of actors and actresses as they sought fame, fortune, and love. Then she felt an eerie chill and she turned to see . . . Caroline.

Le Petit Théâtre, French for "Little Theater," occupies land designated as the original city of Nouvelle Orleans and now known as the French Quarter. The structure at the corner of St. Peter and Chartres Streets was designed by renowned French architect Gilberto Guillemard in 1789 and built in 1794 by Jean Baptiste Orso, a wealthy New Orleans benefactor. Before the year was out, however, on December 8, 1794, a major fire ravaged the city, destroying 212 buildings. This fire followed on the heels of the 1788 Good Friday fire that had burned more than eight hundred homes and public buildings. The French Quarter was in virtual ruins, and nearly all homes and businesses were destroyed or badly damaged except those few structures hugging the Mississippi River bank and, miraculously, the Ursuline Convent.

After these two devastating fires, the French Quarter was architecturally changed forever. Spain was now in control of New Orleans as a result of the secret Treaty of Fountainbleu, ending the Seven Years' War. The rebuilding that took place transformed the area from an old-style French town to a modern Spanish city. Spanish-style baked tile and quarried slate replaced cypress-shingled roofs. The galleried town houses of the French period became narrow Spanish town homes with inner courtyards and decorative ironwork. Buildings set at the sidewalk were made of brick with preventive firewalls. Orso's newly constructed building was destroyed in the fire, but in 1797 it was rebuilt as the residence of the last Spanish governor of Louisiana, Don Manuel Gayoso de Lemos, who was famous for his edict declaring Catholicism as the official faith of the colony. He died of yellow fever in 1799.

The building's history is vague, but it served the expanding city for more than a hundred years. Since it was positioned on the edge of Jackson Square, the structure saw its share of elegant life, political power, and devastating sadness. Ravaged by Civil War occupation, deadly yellow fever epidemics, and the disintegration of inner cities, the property eventually fell into disrepair.

In 1916, a group of amateur actors, under the guidance of Mrs. James Oscar Nixon, formed the Drawing Room Players. This theatrical group got its name because performances were held in the drawing room of fellow founder Mrs. Abraham Goldberg's home on Seventh Street in the Garden District. The troupe's performances were well received and well attended, and this humble space soon became inadequate for the performances, which were gaining in popularity. The company rented a small space in the Lower Pontalba Building facing Jackson Square and continued its theatrical offerings to the community. The famous Anglo-Irish playwright, Lord Dunsany, visiting the city in November 1919, was on hand to formally christen the new playhouse. He dedicated the space "to art" and kicked off the upcoming theatrical season, which would feature his works.

Bolstered by the ever-growing support from local theater-lovers, the group began to look for an even larger space and, in 1922, it purchased land on St. Peter Street. First on the agenda to make the property more conducive to its mission as a community theater was the removal of three dilapidated structures facing Jackson Square. Here the present theater building was erected, designed by the famed architect Richard Koch in the old Spanish Colonial style to complement other French Quarter buildings.

The corner building, dating back to 1797, had been left intact, though in bad shape. This historic structure was saved and in 1963 was renovated to complete the theater's collection of buildings, reception rooms, offices, and dressing rooms, as well as the Children's Corner Theatre that accommodates more than 120 guests.

Legend has it that Caroline, an actress performing at the theater in the early 1920s, had a bright future. She was only twenty-two years old, but she had already proven her artistic skills in several productions. But love was to supersede ambition. The young girl was involved with a veteran actor who was performing at the theater. In fact, they had agreed to meet on the balcony before the play began, perhaps to fuel their flames of passion, perhaps there was another motive. There is no explanation how, but Caroline fell from the balcony to the hard, cold slate below. The acting troupe heard the scream and ran to the courtyard. Caroline was dead; she would be missed. But her spirit never left the theater; perhaps she wants one last scene, one final performance. Caroline is a friendly ghost, and many people have seen her wearing a traditional wedding gown as well as theatrical costumes. She still takes her acting roles seriously and often sports various hairstyles of the parts she played onstage. Caroline has a job at the theater. She is in charge of finding lost or misplaced props. When something appears to be missing or lost, a crew member will call out for Caroline to help find the object, which she does, in time for the curtain to go up.

Caroline is especially helpful because Sigmund likes to hide things. Sigmund, described as short and muscular, was a stage carpenter who is said to have died in the theater. He delights in hiding objects and playing jokes on cast and crew members. His ghost is seen in many areas of the theater and often only parts of him appear. Patrons have described hands on their shoulders and lower legs in boots walking backstage. Sigmund likes to create confusion whenever he can. When a curtain was found snagged on a hook twenty feet above the stage, everyone knew Sigmund had done it. A favorite trick of his is to appear "real" as he engages theatergoers in conversation. Another favorite ghost at Le Petit is Señor Alejandro Venegas, also called the Captain. This elderly Spanish gentleman with a black mustache is a patron of the theater. He attends performances frequently and dresses in nineteenth-century formal wear. He always sits in the same spot in the balcony, front row, second seat on the right aisle. Ticket holders are surprised to find this character from a bygone era sitting, proud as punch, in their seat, but by the time they get back from complaining about the mistake, he is gone, just as the manager had assured them he would be. There are several possibilities as to why Venegas haunts the theater, but, because of his antique dress, it is believed that he died in the building when it was the home of the Spanish governor, Gayoso, and then, more than a century later, he fell in love with an actress when the site became home to the theater group. In any case, ghostly Señor Venegas loves the theater and continues to support the arts . . . and young actresses, even today.

Le Petit is one of the oldest continuously operating community theaters in the United States. The playhouse is equipped with professional lighting, state-of-the art sound equipment, and well-furnished dressing rooms. The main theater has a seating capacity of 450. All the performers at Le Petit are volunteers, according to its community theater charter rules, but many guest artists and professional performers have worked here as well. Ellen DeGeneres, comedian, TV talk show host, and New Orleans native, referred to her connection to Le Petit early in her career in a website post in 2009. Other stars connected to Le Petit are Harry Connick Jr. and Wynton Marsalis. The Tennessee Williams Festival continues to call Le Petit its home.

Gina loved exploring the nooks and crannies of the old buildings, but this morning she had been on a mission. Climbing the narrow backstage stairs, she stood overlooking the lush courtyard that the theater buildings kept safe and out of sight from passersby on the busy French Quarter streets. Here she waited until she felt the cool air rush over her shoulders despite the hot and humid weather, so typical of March in New Orleans. She had visited with the anticipated apparition many times before. Within seconds Caroline appeared on the balcony dressed in the flowing, white wedding gown costume she was to wear for her opening scene the night she died. *Yes,* thought Gina, *the theater is indeed a mysterious place.* She shivered just a second but could not take her eyes from the young actress's emotional spirit. Then Caroline vanished as quickly as she had appeared. Gina did a quick pirouette in honor of her love of dancing and headed down the stairs to meet her cousin Pam. It would be a great festival this year, and she would like to think that Tennessee Williams himself would approve of her annual visit backstage.

Appendix A

Haunted Places to Visit

Andrew Jackson Hotel
919 Royal St.
Once a boys' school, it is haunted by the children who died in a fire here.

The Anne Rice House
1239 First St.
A previous owner haunts the house where financial ruin led to suicide.

Antoine's
713 St. Louis St.
Antoine himself is on hand to make sure guests get the best food, wine, and service.

Arnaud's
813 Bienville St.
Both Arnaud and his flamboyant daughter keep watch over the crowded dining rooms.

Beauregard-Keyes House
1113 Chartres St.
The spirit of a famous Civil War general relives gruesome and bloody battles.

Bourbon Orleans Hotel
717 Orleans St.
The ghost of a dashing Southern gentleman kisses the hands of beautiful young women.

Brennan's Restaurant
417 Royal St.
Haunted by chefs and employees who can't leave the fabulous dining rooms.

The Cabildo
701 Chartres St.
Ghosts of dead soldiers roam the halls in pain and swing from gallows ropes.

1891 Castle Inn
1539 Fourth St.
Haunted by a servant who suffocated and a little girl who fell into a pond and died.

Chalmette Battlefield
Six miles southeast of New Orleans
Veteran war spirits, including Union soldiers, rest restlessly here.

Columns Hotel
3811 St. Charles Ave.
A well-dressed, dapper gentleman checks up on guests, and a child wanders the third floor.

Commander's Palace
1403 Washington Ave.
Owner Emile roams the dining rooms to ensure his guests are treated right.

Cornstalk Hotel
915 Royal St.
A blind ghost haunting the property wanders into places he should not be.

Court of Two Sisters
613 Royal St.
Eerie paranormal phenomena are common at this well-known eatery.

Dauphine Orleans Hotel
415 Dauphine St.
More than one friendly ghost haunts the hotel and May Baily's Bar looking for a good time.

Destrehan Plantation
13034 River Rd. (Destrehan)
Jean Lafitte has been spotted here keeping a watchful eye over his hidden loot.

Devil's Mansion
1319 St. Charles Ave.
The devil himself kept his exotic mistress here until the decay and ruin forced him to leave.

Dueling Oaks
New Orleans City Park
Creole gentlemen who lost their lives defending their honor roam silently under the ancient oaks.

Faulkner House Books
624 Pirate's Alley
Faulkner is said to still smoke his pipe and visit with earlier ghosts who live here.

Flanagan's Pub
625 St. Philip St.
Angela committed suicide in the ladies' room, and her ghost is a regular here.

Gallier Hall
545 St. Charles Ave.
A poltergeist opens and closes toilet stalls and noisily kicks trash bins around.

Griffon House
1447 Constance St.
Civil War soldiers died in a suicide pact but can't cross over to rest in peace.

Hotel Monteleone
214 Royal St.
A conscientious ghost checks the antique grandfather clock in the lobby day and night.

Hotel Provincial
1024 Chartres St.
A Confederate soldier rues his days spent in this former Royal Military Hospital.

Jackson Barracks Military Museum
6400 St. Claude Ave.
Lingering ghosts of General Custer's cavalry stay close to their headstones.

Jefferson Davis Haunted House
2362 Camp St.
The ghost of Jefferson Davis has been seen here where he died a recluse.

Lafayette Cemetery
Prytania Street, across from Commander's Palace
Many Garden District souls and zombies haunt the cemetery.

Lafitte's Blacksmith Shop
941 Bourbon St.
A bearded spirit haunts the old building. Is it Jean Lafitte himself?

Lafitte Guest House
1003 Bourbon St.
A ghostly mother cries for her child taken by yellow fever.

The Lalaurie Mansion
1140 Royal St.
One of the most haunted houses in the city; the site of brutal slave torture.

Lamothe House Hotel
621 Esplanade Ave.
Ghosts of children laugh late at night while their mother searches for them.

Lanaux Mansion
547 Esplanade Ave.
This residence is watched over by a ghostly former owner who loved in silence.

Le Pavillon Hotel
833 Poydras St.
Called "The Belle of New Orleans" and home to many centuries-old ghosts.

Le Petit Théâtre
616 St. Peter St.
Caroline continues to play her part as a desperate woman who loved and lost.

Louisiana Supreme Court Building
400 Royal St.
Murdered witnesses are forever tied to the courthouse waiting to be called to the stand.

Madame John's Legacy
632 Dumaine St.
Home of famous pirate Rene Beluche, who lords over the establishment.

Magnolia Mansion
2127 Prytania St.
Ghosts remain behind after two funerals and often appear as ghostly orbs in photos.

Marie Laveau's House
1020 St. Ann St.
Home of the Voodoo Queen, who died here, but her magic did not.

Metairie Cemetery
5100 Pontchartrain Blvd.
Site of Josie Arlington's infamous "Flaming Tomb" and roaming statue.

The Morgue
626 St. Philip St.
Various angry ghosts still haunt the building, though it stands vacant at the present time.

Napoleon House
500 Chartres St.
Wounded Civil War soldiers replay their time at the former infirmary, once on the second floor.

New Orleans Pharmacy Museum
514 Chartres St.
Grotesque victims of Dr. Dupas's bizarre medical experiments haunt this historic building.

O'Flaherty's Irish Channel Pub
508 Toulouse St.
Angelique seeks her plaçage master, lover, and murderer in death.

Old Absinthe House
240 Bourbon St.
The pirate Jean Lafitte lingers here, still planning the Battle of New Orleans.

Old Ursuline Convent
1112 Chartres St.
Ghostly nuns in religious habits care for the sick and dying who cannot cross to the other world.

Old US Mint
400 Esplanade Ave.
Ghostly employees of the mint enjoy a cigarette or two before vanishing.

Omni Royal Orleans Hotel
621 St. Louis St.
A dutiful maid here tucks guests tightly in bed . . . perhaps, too tightly.

Ormond Plantation
13786 River Rd. (Destrehan)
The curse of a vengeful slave, beaten by his owner, still shrouds this plantation.

Pat O'Brien's
718 St. Peter St.
Ghosts tickle the ivories and party with guests.

Place d'Armes Hotel
625 St. Ann St.
A little girl wanders around the fifth floor, just as she has been doing for 150 years.

Pirate's Alley
Between the St. Louis Cathedral and the Cabildo
Meeting place for nefarious tradesmen who dealt in illegal liquor, slaves, guns, and booty.

The Pontchartrain
2031 St. Charles Ave.
Ghosts of once-wealthy reclusive old sisters gossip together on the ninth floor.

Preservation Hall
726 St. Peter St.
Ghostly trombones and saxophones serenade music lovers.

Prytania Inn
1507 Prytania St.
A child ghost named Isabel relives her tragically fatal fall.

Rodrigue Gallery (Julie's Spirit)
730 Royal St.
The gallery at 730 Royal Street has taken over the 732 Royal Street section where Julie froze to death on the roof.

Royal Café
700 Royal St.
Madam LaBranche still reigns over this most photographed house in the French Quarter.

St. Anthony's Garden
Royal Street, behind the St. Louis Cathedral
At this favorite place for duels, the spirits of those killed for love and honor remain trapped in time.

St. Louis Cemetery No. 1
St. Louis and Basin Streets
The most haunted cemetery in the United States and the resting place of Marie Laveau.

St. Vincent's Guest House
1507 Magazine St.
Ghosts of orphans who died of yellow fever have no place else to go.

Sausage Man
725 Ursulines St.
A sausage maker gets rid of his wife by grinding her up, and then is haunted by his evil deed.

Sultan's Palace
716 Dauphine St.
Site of a horrendous massacre of a sultan and his harem.

Villa Convento Guest House
621 Ursulines St.
"The House of the Rising Sun" ladies still visit regularly.

Appendix B

Further Reading and Investigating

BOOKS

Étouffée, Mon Amour: The Great Restaurants of New Orleans by Kerri McCaffety. A wonderful book about fine food and exquisite dining experiences in New Orleans with a lot of history thrown in for good measure.

Fabulous New Orleans by Lyle Saxon. Saxon recounts his personal impressions of a bygone period in New Orleans and adds some historical facts to his timeless stories.

The French Quarter: An Informal History of the New Orleans Underworld by Herbert Asbury. So much information and so many details are contained in Asbury's easy-to-read stories of a city with a shady past.

The French Quarter of New Orleans by Jim Frasier. Jim Frasier and photographer West Freeman's coffee-table book is chock full of architectural and historical information, and the photography is stunning.

Ghost Hunter's Guide to New Orleans by Jeff Dwyer. Dwyer tells many tales of ghosts and the supernatural; some stories have a new twist that readers may find interesting.

Ghost Stories of Louisiana by Dan Asfar. The author covers a lot of history and many ghostly characters in this enjoyable book about the spirits that continue to live in the most haunted city in the country.

Ghost Stories of Old New Orleans by Jeanne deLavigne. This book, considered a "must read" by those who study paranormal phenomena, presents the major characters and places in the ghostly world of New Orleans.

Gumbo Ya-Ya: A Collection of Louisiana Folk Tales by Robert Tallant and Lyle Saxon. This fantastic collection of Cajun and Creole folklore told by beguiling raconteurs is a treasure trove of entertainment.

Haunted New Orleans: History & Hauntings of the Crescent City and *Haunted New Orleans: Ghosts & Hauntings of the Crescent City* by Troy Taylor. The author covers stories not found in other books about ghosts in New Orleans.

Old New Orleans: A History of the Vieux Carré, Its Ancient and Historical Buildings by Stanley Clisby Arthur. This author in the past delves into the past and brings old New Orleans to life.

New Orleans Ghosts (1993), *New Orleans Ghosts II* (1999), and *New Orleans Ghosts III* (2004) by Victor C. Klein. Many of these ghost stories are documented, and multiple resources are used for authentication.

The World from Jackson Square: A New Orleans Reader edited by Etolia S. Basso. Basso has compiled essays and informational excerpts from historic and literary sources chronicling the early eras of New Orleans.

WEB RESOURCES

A guide by the Federal Writers' Project of the Works Progress Administration for the city of New Orleans offers an in-depth historical reference for many places, people, and events. www.archive.org/details/neworleanscity00writmiss

Hauntedhovel.com. This site offers lots of information, plenty to read, and many places and stories to explore. www.hauntedhovel.com/hauntedlouisiana

Haunted New Orleans Tours. All the information you need about the various haunted tours available in New Orleans can be found here. http://hauntedneworleanstours.com

The History of New Orleans by John Kendall. This is a great historical reference of New Orleans people and places. http://penelope.uchicago.edu/Thayer/E/Gazetteer/Places/America/United_States/Louisiana/New_Orleans/_Texts/KENHNO/home.html

The International Society for Paranormal Research, ISPR. This is the official site for the ISPR and provides lots of interesting information about ghosts and paranormal activities. http://ispr.net/

New Orleans ghost tour information can also be found at www.neworleansghosts.com

Nola.com. Primary and up-to-date resource for New Orleans news, history, and tales of ghosts and vampires. Use the search button. www.nola.com

Appendix C
References

Adcock, Andrea, and Robert Cleveland. "Did Hurricane Katrina Scare the Spooks Away from the Big Easy?" *Alternate Perceptions Magazine,* 141, October 2009. www.mysterious-america.net/bigeasyghosts.html (accessed October 1, 2011).

Arthur, Stanley Clisby. *Old New Orleans: A History of the Vieux Carré, Its Ancient and Historical Buildings.* New Orleans, LA: Harmanson, 1946.

Antoine's Restaurant. www.antoines.com (accessed July 15, 2011).

Arnaud's Restaurant. www.arnaudsrestaurant.com (accessed September 5, 2011).

Asbury, Herbert. *The French Quarter: An Informal History of the New Orleans Underworld.* New York, NY: Alfred A. Knopf Inc., 1936.

Asfar, Dan. *Ghost Stories of Louisiana.* Auburn, WA: Lone Pine Publishing International, 2007.

Basso, Etolia S., ed. *The World from Jackson Square: A New Orleans Reader.* New York, NY: Farrar, Straus and Company, 1948.

Bizier, Richard, and Roch Nadeau. *New Orleans*. Gretna, LA: Pelican Publishing Company, 1998.

Bourbon Orleans Hotel. www.bourbonorleans.com (accessed September 3, 2011).

Cathedral-Basilica of St. Louis, King of France. http://stlouiscathedral.org/ (accessed August 3, 2011).

Columns Hotel. www.thecolumns.com (accessed August 1, 2011).

Commander's Palace. www.commanderspalace.com (accessed July 10, 2011).

Cowan, Walter G., Charles L. Dufour, and O. K. Leblanc. *New Orleans Yesterday and Today: A Guide to the City*. Baton Rouge: Louisiana State University Press, 2001.

deLavigne, Jeanne. *Ghost Stories of Old New Orleans*. New York, NY: Rinehart & Company Inc., 1946.

Dureau, Lorena. "Sultan's House, Life with an Exotic Ghost." *Times-Picayune,* 200+, February 11, 1979.

Dwyer, Jeff. *Ghost Hunter's Guide to New Orleans*. Gretna, LA: Pelican Publishing Company, 2007.

"Federal Writers' Project of the Works Progress Administration for the City of New Orleans." New Orleans City Guide. Boston, MA: Houghton Mifflin Co., 1938. www.archive.org/details/neworleanscity00writmiss (accessed August 5, 2011).

Frasier, Jim. *The French Quarter of New Orleans*. Jackson: University Press of Mississippi, 2003.

Hauntedhovel.com. "Ever Been Spooked? Why Not Tell Us about It and Submit a Ghost Story!" www.hauntedhovel .com/submitaghoststory.html (accessed October 23, 2011).

Haunted New Orleans Tours. "Haunted New Orleans: Top Ten Haunted Hotels." www.hauntedneworleanstours .com/toptenhaunted/toptenhauntednolahotels/ (accessed September 5, 2011).

Hotel Monteleone. http://hotelmonteleone.com (accessed July 15, 2011).

Hotel Provincial. www.hotelprovincial.com (accessed July 15, 2011).

Huber, Leonard Victor. *New Orleans: A Pictorial History*. Gretna, LA: Pelican Publishing Company, 1991.

Kendall, John. *The History of New Orleans*. Chicago, IL: The Lewis Publishing Company, 1922. http://penelope. uchicago.edu/Thayer/E/Gazetteer/Places/America/ United_States/Louisiana/New_Orleans/_Texts/KENHNO/ home.html (accessed July 27, 2011).

Klein, Victor C. *New Orleans Ghosts*. Chapel Hill, NC: Lycanthrope Press, 1993.

———. *New Orleans Ghosts II*. Metairie, LA: Lycanthrope Press, 1999.

———. *New Orleans Ghosts III*. Metairie, LA: Lycanthrope Press, 2004.

Kmen, Henry A. *Music in New Orleans: The Formative Years, 1791–1841*. Baton Rouge: Louisiana State University Press, 1966.

Lanier, Gina. "New Orleans: The Most Haunted Paranormal Place in the United States . . . Possibly the World!" www .ginalanier.com/hauntedplaces.php (accessed October 4, 2011).

Lasky, Jane. "Haunted Hotel: New Orleans's Monteleone Hosts Ghosts (Proof Here)." Examiner.com. www.examiner.com/travel-in-los-angeles/haunted-hotel-new-orleans-s-monteleone-hosts-ghosts-proof-here#ixzz1ZqGFoUn5 (accessed August 20, 2011).

Laughlin, Clarence John. *Ghosts along the Mississippi*. Jackson: University Press of Mississippi, 1988.

Le Petit Théâtre du Vieux Carré. www.lepetittheatre.com (accessed June 6, 2011).

McCaffety, Kerri. *Étouffée, Mon Amour: The Great Restaurants of New Orleans.* Gretna, LA: Pelican Publishing Company, 2002.

New Orleans Pharmacy Museum. www.pharmacymuseum.org (accessed July 15, 2011).

Old New Orleans. "All in a Row: Three St. Peter Street Neighbors." www.old-new-orleans.com/NO_Neighbors .html (accessed October 15, 2011).

Olsen, Debbie. "Ghost-Hunting in New Orleans, a 'Parapsychology Expedition.'" RedDeerAdvocate.com. October 31, 2009. www.reddeeradvocate.com/lifestyles/ Ghosthunting_in_New_Orleans_a_parapsychology_ expedition_67742187.html (accessed October 10, 2011).

Pat O'Brien's. www.patobriens.com/patobriens (accessed October 1, 2011).

Preservation Hall. www.preservationhall.com/hall/index. aspx (accessed October 9, 2011).

Rose, Christopher. "Invasion of the Tourist Snatchers: The Quarter Scary-Tour Business Has Turned Cutthroat." Nola.com. June 13, 1997. www.nola.com/haunted/ vampires/061397tour.html (accessed October 9, 2011).

Saxon, Lyle. *Fabulous New Orleans*. Gretna, LA: Pelican Publishing Company, 1995.

The Shadowlands. "Haunted Places in Louisiana." http://theshadowlands.net/places/louisiana.htm (accessed October 8, 2011).

Sillery, Barbara. *The Haunting of Louisiana*. Gretna, LA: Pelican Publishing, 2001.

Smith, Kalila Katherina. *Journey into Darkness: Ghosts and Vampires of New Orleans*. Third edition. New Orleans, LA: DeSimeon Publications, Third Edition, 1998.

Tallant, Robert, and Lyle Saxon. *Gumbo Ya-Ya: A Collection of Louisiana Folk Tales*. Third edition. Gretna, LA: Pelican Publishing, 1991.

Taylor, Troy. *Haunted New Orleans: History & Hauntings of the Crescent City*. Charleston, SC: Haunted America, a division of the History Press, 2011.

_____. *Haunted New Orleans: Ghosts & Hauntings of the Crescent City*. Alton, IL: Whitechapel Productions Press, 2000.

Toledano, Roulhac. *The National Trust Guide to New Orleans: The Definitive Guide to Architectural and Cultural Treasures*. New York, NY: John Wiley & Sons, 1996.

Turnage, Sheila. *Haunted Inns of the Southeast.* Winston-Salem, NC: John F. Blair, 2001.

Wilson, Samuel, Jr. "Maspero's Exchange: Its Predecessors and Successors," *Louisiana History: The Journal of the Louisiana Historical Association,* Vol. 30, No. 2 (Spring 1989), pp. 191–220.

About the Author

Bonnye E. Stuart is a ninth-generation New Orleanian and a member of the very large Perret family. She grew up in the city amid Mamma, Grandma and Grandpa, thirty-nine first cousins, and lots of aunts and uncles. Her four children were all born in New Orleans as tenth-generation Perret children. Last year an eleventh-generation boy made his appearance in New Orleans. Stuart got her bachelor's degree in advertising from the Manship School of Journalism at Louisiana State University—go Tigers!—and earned her master's degree in communication at the University of New Orleans. She writes short stories, poems, and plays, many of which are based on her life and family in New Orleans, and currently teaches at Winthrop University in South Carolina.